Come to Be Killed

Come to Be Killed

E. X. FERRARS

PUBLISHED FOR THE CRIME CLUB BY
DOUBLEDAY & COMPANY, INC.
GARDEN CITY, NEW YORK
1987

FER

All of the characters in this book
are fictitious, and any resemblance
to actual persons, living or dead,
is purely coincidental.

Library of Congress Cataloging-in-Publication Data

Ferrars, E. X.
Come to be killed.

I. Title.
PR6003.R458C6 1987   823'.912   86–32783
ISBN 0-385-24199-2

Come to Be Killed

CHAPTER 1

There was no one at the airport to meet Rachel Gairdner.

It took her about half an hour to convince herself of it. At first she was sure that her brother was somewhere there among the crowd gathered outside the exit, waiting for friends and relatives to emerge, and that he had simply not seen her as she stood waiting.

Then she thought that he would soon arrive, full of apologies, of course, for being late. Not that it was like him to be late. He was a punctilious young man, far less casual about such things as time, money or commitments generally than she was herself. So inevitably she began to think that something must have happened to him.

Either his car would not start, or he had been in an accident, or he had been taken suddenly ill.

But he was never taken ill. He had the unobtrusive sort of good health that gets taken so for granted that even a common cold seems out of character. And if his car would not start, surely he would have had the sense to take a taxi rather than fail to meet her. And it was unthinkable that he should simply have made a mistake about the day on which she was to arrive.

So it began to seem most unpleasantly probable that he had been in an accident.

The sun beat down on Rachel out of a sky of deepest blue. She felt almost ready to cry from sheer fatigue, and the winter clothes that she had had to wear for the start of the journey from London in a peculiarly bitter January felt heavy and moistly clinging in the Australian morning. She had flown direct from Heathrow to Adelaide without breaking the journey, and even though she had flown first class, her body ached and her mind was confused by tiredness.

She had never flown first class before and she felt an absurd sort of guilt at having treated herself to the luxury of it on this occasion. She was one of the people, she felt, who naturally travelled tourist. But that was simply because she had not yet become accustomed to the fact that she was a rich woman. It was a more difficult adjustment to make than she would have expected. Old habits, it would seem, died hard. She had not yet bought any expensive clothes, or an expensive car, or thought of staying in any good hotels. This trip to visit Ian, who had been working in Adelaide for two years, had been her first cautious venture into the world of the wealthy.

The relatively wealthy, that was to say. To a young woman who had been working for several years as a teacher of history in a school in Edinburgh, it felt as if she had indeed come into riches when her aunt Christina died and left her all of which she was possessed. But still, Rachel would never, for instance, think of buying a Rolls-Royce, or diamonds, or of having a swimming-pool. It was not in her nature to do so. She would like to see a little of the world before she grew much older and she had given up her teaching job and had thoughts of buying herself a cottage in the Highlands, but she did not really want to change the way of living to which she was accustomed. Meanwhile, she just possibly might stay on in Australia for a time if she and Ian turned out to be as good friends as they had been when they were younger.

Only now he was not at the airport to meet her. What was she to do about it?

The answer was that she must take a taxi and go to his lodgings, in which he had been able to take a room for her.

Finding a taxi, she gave the address, 21 Bessborough

Street, which she knew was in a suburb of Adelaide called Betty Hill, and trying to control her fears about what might have happened to him, she settled herself to take a first look at the small portion ahead of her of this unfamiliar continent.

But she could not stop her eyes closing. Every little while she forced them to open and caught glimpses of neat bungalows in gardens full of roses, of walls draped with great clusters of bougainvillaea, and of occasional trees smothered in splendid scarlet blossoms. And over all there was a sky so richly blue that there was something almost improbable about it. But her weariness and her fears about Ian kept returning and made her want to shut out everything else.

After all, terrible things did happen to people. There was no reason to think that one was immune to calamity.

The taxi stopped after what seemed a long time in front of a small modern bungalow in a garden that looked curiously shabby in comparison with those on either side of it. The grass of its small lawn was ragged and burnt brown by the sun. Sleazy-looking shrubs overhung the uneven paved path to the door.

Rachel stumbled out of the taxi, catching a glimpse as she did so of the sea at the far end of the road, and began fumbling through the unfamiliar currency in her handbag for the eleven dollars and thirty cents that the driver told her the trip had cost her. In the end she simply held out to him a handful of money and he helped himself out of it, and after carrying her suitcase to the door of the bungalow, wished her a happy stay in Australia and drove off.

She went up to the door and rang the bell.

At that time Rachel was twenty-nine and had a feeling that this was virtually middle age. So much time had passed without much happening to her. She had once almost got married but had eluded it at the last moment. She had had one fairly long-lasting love affair and had been relieved when it had quietly died of its own accord without recriminations on either side. She had been a successful teacher, popular with her pupils and her colleagues, but her heart had never been in her work. At some time in her life, she thought, she had taken a wrong step, coming to accept the fact that some degree of frustration was to be her lot and that this was probably normal in the lives of most people.

Yet she looked a young woman of lively charm and generally she made friends easily. She was small and slim and bright-faced. She had very large brown eyes which at times could appear attentively observant and at others almost disconcertingly absent-minded, and she had a wide forehead, high cheekbones and a small, pointed chin. Her hair was dark and curly. This morning she had forgotten to comb it and in the tweed skirt and quilted jacket that she had worn for the journey she looked uncharacteristically tousled and unkempt, a look that was exaggerated by her expression of fatigue and anxiety.

The bell was answered by a loud barking of dogs. Then the door was opened by a short, thin young man with dark hair and sharp aquiline features. He was wearing a T-shirt and jeans. He gave her a blank look, as if he had no idea who she was or what she might be doing there, while two dogs rushed out of the house, both of them barking wildly at Rachel. One was a boxer, the other a short-legged animal of indeterminate breed.

"Mr. Constoupolis?" she said. She knew that that was the name of Ian's landlord and that he was a Greek. "I'm Rachel Gairdner. I believe you're expecting me."

The man's thin face cracked open in a sudden smile that showed a great many excellent teeth. He held out a hand.

"Miss Gairdner—yes!" he said. Then he shouted furiously at the dog. "Be quiet, you! Be quiet!" He turned his smile once more on Rachel. "Come in, come in. We weren't sure if you would come. We didn't know what to expect. This is your luggage?"

Rachel said that it was and let him carry her suitcase into the bungalow for her.

He took her along a passage empty of furniture and with no carpet on the bare boards of its floor. At some time in the past the walls had been painted white, but that must have been a fair while ago, for now they were dingy and discoloured. He flung open a door.

"Here is your room," he said. "I hope you like it."

The dogs had followed them in, sniffing at Rachel's heels, then thrusting their way into the room ahead of her and proceeding to investigate it, as if to make sure that it was suitable for her.

"Thank you," she said, going in.

It was a small room into which the sunshine could hardly enter through the thick creeper hanging outside the window. There was cheap modern furniture in the room but it looked comfortable enough, though, as the empty corridor had done, it gave Rachel an odd sense of something temporary, something hardly lived in.

"Is my brother here?" she asked.

"Your brother—ah yes, of course, your brother." Mr. Constoupolis drew a hand down the side of his face. "I'll call Maria," he said. "You'll want some coffee."

He spoke English with a strong Australian accent and with only a faint trace in it of the country of his origin.

"So my brother *is* here," Rachel said. "Then what's the matter with him? Is he ill?"

"Ah no, he's not *here*, not today. And he was not at the airport, eh? Is that right?"

"No, he wasn't there." With every moment Rachel's anxiety was mounting. "What d'you mean, he isn't *here?* Where is he?"

"I wish I could tell you. I'll call Maria."

Before Rachel could ask him to explain himself, he

slipped out of the room and Rachel heard him calling, "Maria, Maria, the girl has come! She wants coffee."

A door somewhere in the bungalow opened and closed and with the sound of sandals slapping on the floor of the passage, a young woman appeared in the doorway of the room.

"You are Rachel?" she said. "Ian's sister?"

So there was to be no formality between them.

She was about Rachel's age, but considerably taller, with big breasts and thick hips and smooth dark skin on a plump oval face. Her straight black hair was pulled tightly back from it and fastened with a knot of pink chiffon. She was wearing a bright pink sleeveless dress that hung loosely on her, almost like a maternity dress, and showed off her fine though heavy shoulders. She had small eyes, as dark as prunes, and a large, soft-lipped mouth.

"Yes, where *is* Ian?" Rachel repeated.

"I wish we knew, dear," Maria answered. "Now take off your coat and come into the lounge and I'll bring some coffee and we'll talk about it."

It made Rachel aware that she was still wearing her coat. She took it off and dropped it on the bed while Maria disappeared to the kitchen to make some coffee.

Accompanied by the dogs, her husband led Rachel into a large room at the front of the bungalow. It had a high ceiling and a luridly coloured square of carpet on the floor and a sparse amount of the same kind of cheap furniture as there had been in the bedroom from which they had just come. It might be, Rachel thought, that the Constoupolis couple had only just moved in and had not yet gone about furnishing the house fully. Yet Ian, she knew, had been lodging with them for about three months.

"Then you don't know yourselves where Ian is this morning, Mr. Constoupolis," she said. "When did you see him last?"

"Call me Alex," he said. "That's my name, like Alexander the Great. My family came from Northern Macedonia too, but I have lived here since I was twenty. Maria is Greek too, but she was born here. Now sit down and make yourself comfortable. You must be very tired."

"But about my brother, Mr. Constoup—Alex," Rachel said. She dropped into a chair and realized only as she did so how shaky she felt. "Please tell me why you think he wasn't at the airport."

"But we don't know, that's the point," he said with a note of exasperation in his voice as if he were becoming impatient with her for her lack of understanding. "Yesterday morning, Friday, he went to work as usual, but he didn't come home in the evening. That didn't mean anything to us. Since he became involved with the young woman, Eudora Linley— But perhaps you don't know about that."

"I know something about it," Rachel answered. "He mentioned meeting her in one of his letters."

"Ah. Yes. Well." Alex Constoupolis sat down and the boxer settled at his feet. The small brown dog sprang up into a chair and slumped down in comfort. "You like dogs?" he asked.

"I like them all right," Rachel said. "But what you're telling me, or trying to avoid telling me, is that you think Ian spent the night with this girl Eudora and just forgot to meet me at the airport. It doesn't sound like him."

"It isn't like him at all!" He smacked his hands down on his knees. They were long, bony hands and the knees inside his jeans gave the impression of being bony. "But what else do you suggest? He went to work yesterday morning and did not come back for his tea in the evening and this morning we saw his bed had not been slept in. So we thought: Ah, it's as we thought with the girl, it's gone as far as that now, but he'll certainly go to the airport to meet his sister. But when you arrive here by yourself we start to wonder . . . You see, we have a problem of our own."

"Concerning Ian?"

"Yes, yes, certainly concerning Ian."

"You don't mean you think he's absconded without paying you some rent he owes you."

"No, no, of course nothing like that. He's a very reliable young man, an altogether admirable tenant. And we're very fond of him. But the girl Eudora: perhaps she's not a good influence. Very beautiful. He's brought her here once or twice. But unstable, I should say, wild, even a little crazy. She might perhaps stop him going to the airport for some strange reason of her own. Jealousy, maybe, if she knows he cares a lot for you. But that's not the problem at the moment. Not our problem. It's the dogs."

"I'm sorry, I don't understand," Rachel said.

"I'll explain . . ."

But before he could do so Maria appeared in the doorway with a tray and coffee.

"I'm afraid I just warmed it up, but it's quite fresh," she said. "We'd only just had our breakfast when you arrived and this was left over. How do you like it—black, cream, sugar?"

Rachel did not much want any coffee at all. She felt that she had been eating and drinking on the plane almost without stopping from the time that it had left Heathrow until it had reached Adelaide. What she did want desperately was a bath. She wanted to get out of her winter clothes, soak comfortably in a bath for a while and then probably go to bed, whether or not to sleep did not matter. She would at least be able to stretch out her cramped limbs and rest for a few hours and get rid of the humming noise of the plane that still reverberated in her ears.

Since hearing of the part that Eudora Linley might have had to play in Ian's failure to meet her, she felt rather less apprehensive than she had before. She had always regarded Ian as a hopeless innocent where women were concerned. He was generally clay in the hands of anyone reasonably attractive who took him sufficiently firmly in hand.

"Black, please," she said, "and no sugar. But if you'd explain about the dogs . . ."

"Yes, yes, of course." Alex massaged his thin knees. "You see, Monday is Australia Day, a holiday. I've time off from my job. I'm a printer, I work for the Adelaide *Clarion*. And we were going to go away tomorrow to visit some friends in Mildura. That's a small town in New South Wales, about four or five hours' drive from here. But we weren't going to drive because we've had to leave our car in the garage. The gearbox is giving trouble. So we were going to fly. And that meant, of course, we couldn't take the dogs and Ian promised us he'd look after them. They're fond of him and he knows their ways and what they need, so it would have been fine. But now that he's gone missing, what can we do, unless, of course . . ." His narrow face cracked across once more in one of his toothy smiles. "You say you like dogs?"

Rachel gave a tired nod, sipping her coffee.

"I'll look after them for you, if that's all that's worrying you," she said. "But if you're right that Ian's with Eudora, he'll turn up sometime today, don't you think?"

"That's right, he will, that's for sure." But Rachel thought that she heard a note of uncertainty in Alex's voice.

"Of course he will," Maria said. She had thrown herself down in a chair that looked a little fragile to support her opulent weight. Her pink dress billowed out around her. Her legs, which were bare and which she had thrust out before her, were plump but shapely. "I believe myself it's the first time he's lost his head about a woman, but he'll wake up and come to his senses by and by. You mustn't worry. Is your coffee as you like it?"

"Thank you, it's very good," Rachel replied. "But would it be possible for me to have a bath now?"

"I'm sorry, we have no bath," Maria said. "Only a shower, but you're welcome to it. And have a good rest after it, for as long as you like. It'll take you some days, I expect, to get used to the difference in time. We're ten hours ahead of you. But you must do just as you please. And if you mean it that you'll look after the dogs so that we can visit our friends after all, we'll be so grateful."

"You must leave me instructions about feeding them and so on," Rachel said. "When are you leaving?"

"On the early-morning flight. It would have been nice to leave today and have the whole weekend in Mildura, but Alex has to work today."

"In fact, I should be getting off to it now." He stood up. "I'll be very late as it is, but I waited in case you were going to turn up and we could arrange something with you about the dogs. I'm so glad you got here safely. See you later." He stopped to give his wife a peck on her forehead and went out.

"Have you tried telephoning Eudora?" Rachel asked Maria as the door closed behind him.

"We don't know her number," Maria replied. "She shares a flat with some friends, I think, and the telephone is in one of their names."

"Couldn't we find it out from some friend of Ian's? He has friends, I suppose."

"Yes, of course, but you know how it is, he calls them Pete and Tony and Bob, but never mentions their surnames. I think Pete is a special friend of his, but I don't know his other name. So it's no use trying to find him in the directory."

"What about his boss?"

Rachel knew that the name of Ian's boss was Andrew Wellman. He was head of the Adelaide office of a firm called Ledyard Groome and Company that manufactured agricultural machinery. It was a British-owned firm, but all its employees here, with the exception of Ian, were Australian. Ian, who had the prospect of promotion at home, had been sent out to study the work of the company in Australia, and then should have gone on to New Zealand and perhaps Canada. But because he had been enjoying himself he had managed to arrange to stay on in Adelaide, at least for longer than had been originally intended. In his letters to Rachel it had been clear that he was very contented and had thought of seeing if he could become part of the permanent establishment.

"We didn't think of that," Maria said. "You see, it was only after you arrived here by yourself that we began to wonder what had happened to Ian. And after all, do you ring a man up to ask him if he knows if one of his staff may have spent the night with his secretary?"

"Is that what she is?"

"Mr. Wellman's secretary, yes."

Rachel shook her head. "I don't understand it. I've a nasty feeling he must have been in an accident, perhaps on his way to the airport this morning. I wonder if we should call the police and ask if any accident's been reported."

"Well, perhaps, but not yet," Maria said with a sudden firmness in her tone that Rachel noticed, but by which her fatigue-fogged mind was only faintly puzzled. "He may walk in at any time and be very annoyed with us if we've made a fuss about him. He doesn't like fuss, you must know that about him. What I think you should do is have a shower, then go to bed and try to stop worrying. Have a good rest and if Ian still isn't here when you wake up, we'll think about what we should do then."

Rachel supposed it was good advice. She was disappointed that she would have to make do with a shower instead of being able to soak in a bath, but it would be better than nothing. She let Maria lead her back to her bedroom, show her where the shower-room was and where her towels hung, and was about to unlock her suitcase when it occurred to her to ask, "Have you looked to see if Ian's things are all in his room, or did he take anything with him yesterday?"

Maria hesitated in the doorway of the bedroom. Rachel could not have said why it was but all of a sudden she felt that there was something hostile in the way the other woman looked at her. Yet she smiled with what was obviously meant to be reassurance.

"The first thing we did this morning when we realized Ian hadn't come home last night was take a look in his room," she said. "We didn't see anything unusual. I couldn't tell you if he took anything away with him because I don't know so much about what he had, but at least his pyjamas are under his pillow and his dressing-gown is hanging on its peg, and his razor and his tooth-brush are in their usual places. I believe that girl Eudora is the explanation of everything. He went home with her, not meaning to spend the night, and then—well, he did. But you'll see, he'll walk in presently."

She went out, leaving Rachel to undress and have her shower.

CHAPTER 2

Rachel had the shower, dug a night-dress out of her suit-case without unpacking it and went to bed.

She did not expect to be able to sleep. A sense of peculiar helplessness, of simply not knowing what she ought to do in the house of these strangers in this strange country, disturbed her. Why had she suddenly started thinking Maria was hostile? Was it just that she thought Rachel was making a fuss about nothing? Probably Maria was right and Ian would soon walk in, repentant but all in one piece.

With these thoughts floating about confusedly in her brain, Rachel after all fell asleep, sinking comfortably into deep unconsciousness.

What wakened her she did not know, except that she heard the dogs barking and thought that she had heard a door closing. Maria, she thought, was probably taking the dogs for a walk and they were barking, as dogs will, in their pleasure at being taken out. Turning over, she was soon sound asleep again.

When she woke again it was more completely. She looked at her watch, only to realize that she had not adjusted it to local time. But certainly, she thought, she ought to get up. And while she was about it, she would unpack and put on a summer dress. Getting out of bed, she opened her suitcase again and started hanging up the dresses that she had brought in the built-in cupboard in the room. She had really brought very little with her. If she needed more, she had thought when she was packing, she could buy it in Adelaide. She would probably enjoy shopping in a strange city.

The house was quiet. There was no sound of any movement in it. Perhaps Maria and the dogs had not yet returned from their walk. It was a curious thing that for a few moments Rachel did not remember that Ian ought certainly to have returned to the house by now. When the thought of this did suddenly occur to her and all her worries about him came flooding back, she felt a shock that made her plunge into the first clothes that came to hand and dart out of the room to look for him.

He was not in the bungalow. Neither was Alex, nor Maria. Nor were the dogs.

Going from room to room, Rachel saw a small electric clock in the sitting-room which told her that the local time was half past three. Adjusting her watch to match it, she went on in her search, knocking on each door before entering the room in case the explanation of the silence was that Maria was lying down, perhaps asleep, and had the dogs with her. But the bedroom that was obviously that of her and Alex was empty. It was in a curious state of disorder, for cupboards as well as drawers were open and a litter of underclothes, shoes, shirts and jeans was scattered on the bed and the floor.

Ian's room was tidy. There were things in it which made Rachel able to identify it as his, some worn paperbacks from which he would never be parted, most of them of Victorian novelists, also a photograph of herself that she had sent him some months earlier, propped up against a mirror on the dressing-table, and a very old silk dressing-gown that she had given him as a Christmas present several years ago which was hanging from a peg on the door.

Besides these things there were others that he must have acquired since coming here, a television set, a hi-fi, a pair of brightly coloured swimming-trunks draped over the back of a chair. Of all the rooms in the house it looked the most lived-in, since the state of the Constoupolises' bedroom gave in a rather desolate air of neglect, almost as if it were never used by anyone.

The kitchen was the last room into which Rachel looked. She was drawn there by a sound of whining outside the back door. She went to it and found that it was locked, but the key was in the lock and she opened it. The boxer was there, impatient to be let in. He thrust past her into the kitchen and went to a bowl on the floor, then looked at her reproachfully because the bowl was empty.

She thought that it must have held water and that what he wanted was a drink. Picking the bowl up, she filled it at the sink and put it down again. As he started to lap eagerly, Rachel stood watching him, thinking that he was a handsome animal, muscular and well-kept. Then she looked out of the open door to see if the other dog was there, but there was no sign of him.

It was evident, however, since the boxer was here, that the dogs had not been taken for a walk. Feeling responsible for them already, though she believed she was not expected to start looking after them until tomorrow, she thought she ought to see if the small brown dog was in the garden. Strolling round the house, she found him stretched in a patch of shade under a straggling shrub. He appeared to be asleep but when she approached him he lifted his head and gave one or two lazy wags of his tail. There seemed no point in disturbing him.

But the gate into the street was open and she thought it best, if the dog was remaining in the garden, to close it. She did so, then returned to the kitchen, and it was only as she did this that she noticed a card, propped up against a bottle of wine, on the plastic-topped table.

The card was addressed to her in a small, hurried-looking scrawl.

Dear Rachel—We are sorry to leave you alone but after all I am free this afternoon so we have decided to go to our friends in Mildura today. I am sure Ian will soon come back and you will like to be together. Please make yourself at home. Maria has put a quiche and salad and fruit and cheese in the refrigerator for your tea. Help yourself to anything you want. I pulled the cork out of this bottle of wine as I thought you might like it. It is quite good. The boxer's name is Bungo and the little one is Charlie. Their food, a tin a day each and some biscuits if they are hungry, is in the cupboard under the window. We are grateful to you for saying you would look after them. They are very friendly dogs and no trouble. Looking forward to seeing you again after the holiday—Alex.

She sat down on one of the chairs at the table. Bungo, the boxer, came over to her, sniffed at her curiously, then laid his head on her lap and gazed up at her sentimentally. She stroked him absent-mindedly behind the ears, which he seemed to like, for when she let her hand drop he prodded her with a paw to go on.

Her big brown eyes had their blank look, as if at the moment she could not bring herself to think coherently about anything. In fact she was thinking of how helplessly alone she was. She had never felt so alone in her life, even when Aunt Christina, with whom she had been living while she was teaching at a school in Edinburgh, had died and Rachel had had her big old Georgian house to herself. For here she was in a strange house, in a strange country, on a strange continent, with a missing brother and abandoned by her hosts. She had no one to advise her what she should do now. She had not a single acquaintance to whom she could turn.

Should she simply help herself to the things in the refrigerator which had been thoughtfully left there for her tea, a meal which she knew in Australia could mean what she would call dinner or perhaps supper, and go on trusting that Ian would presently walk in? Or should she look up the telephone number of Andrew Wellman in the directory and see if he had any information about Ian?

After all, it was not certain that he had spent the night with his girl-friend. He might have been sent away from Adelaide sometime during the last few days on some business errand about which his boss would know, and somehow had been held up and unable to return. That began to seem to Rachel the most probable thing to have happened. Only if he had, if his car had broken down or some aeroplane flight on which he had been counting had been cancelled, why had he not telephoned the Constoupolises?

That was what he would surely have done unless he was actually incapable of it. That was to say, unless he had been in an accident, had been hurt, had even . . .

She gave a sharp shudder and her eyes lost their faraway expression, changing to one of dark intensity. Unless he had even been killed.

Once more she began to think of calling the police to ask if any accident had been reported. But as she thought of doing this a strange recollection came to her. It was of what she had believed was a sudden mood of hostility in Maria which had begun, Rachel was almost sure, after her suggestion that she should call the police. But she thought now that that could not be right. Why should Maria have anything against her doing that? And the feeling that she had suddenly become hostile could have been a complete mistake. She might simply have been impatient, occupied with concerns of her own, and perhaps irritated with Ian for leaving her uncertain about what she ought to do about the all-important dogs. Anyway, these considerations did not affect the question of whether Rachel should call the police now. On the whole she thought that it would be the best thing to do.

But first she rather liked the idea of having a drink. It would help to allay her nervousness and probably make her talk more lucidly to the policeman who answered her. Getting up, she found a wineglass in a cupboard, went back to the kitchen table and was just about to pull the cork out of the bottle of wine when she heard a loud barking and yelping in the garden, then, shrilly and loudly, the ringing of the front-door bell.

CHAPTER 3

Rachel's first thought was that of course it was Ian. But even as she ran towards the door she wondered why it was that he had no key of his own.

Bungo reached the door ahead of her, growling and snarling. So she was prepared for the fact, by the time she opened the door, that it would not be Ian who had rung the bell. For Bungo must know Ian well by now and might have greeted him with excited barking, but not with such a sound of canine animus.

It was as she opened the door that she became aware of something that she had been too involved in her own immediate problems to notice before. It was that the air was filled with the sound of an enormous voice, coming from somewhere outside, booming and reverberating in the stillness of the afternoon. From somewhere not very far away someone was speaking into a microphone that magnified his voice fantastically. It sounded as if some giant had arrived on the beach near at hand and was preaching the inhabitants of Betty Hill a sermon. She could not make out any particular words, but it was plain from the rhythm of it that the giant was making a speech. Then all of a sudden there was music, as outsize as the voice had been.

Of course, it was a holiday, she remembered, and some sort of festival must be in progress.

She opened the door.

A tall man stood there. He was broad as well as tall, with a great paunch, the size of which was exaggerated by the belt that he was wearing under it to hold up his crumpled trousers and which outlined the unsightly bulge. He had a big square head with a wide face, in the centre of which his features looked curiously small and crushed together. He had small sharp eyes of greenish-grey and bushy brown eyebrows. His hair was a light brown and crisply curly, going grey at the temples. His age was about forty.

He looked as if he found it as surprising to see Rachel there as she did to see him.

"Constoupolis?" he said questioningly.

"I'm afraid he isn't here," she answered.

"Mrs. Constoupolis, then?"

"No, she isn't here either."

"Neither of them here?"

"No."

"But where are they then?"

The music was shattering the quiet of the afternoon. Rachel had never been able to endure loud noises and it increased the confusion in her mind which she seemed to have been feeling ever since she had arrived here.

"I'm not quite sure," she replied, thinking that she wanted to know more about this man before she told him anything, even about the fact that the Constoupolis couple had suddenly taken off on a visit to friends. "Do you mind telling me who you are?"

"Who are you, if it comes to that?" His voice was harsh and though she was not familiar with the subtleties of the Australian accent, she thought it was not that of a cultured man.

"My name's Gairdner," she said. "I'm a visitor."

"Oh, Gairdner," he said, as if that meant something to him. "Some relation of the bloke who's been living here?"

"He's my brother, but he isn't in either, if you want to see him, and I'm not sure when he'll be back. And you still haven't told me who you are."

"My name's Slattery, not that that'll mean anything to

you. And I want to see Constoupolis. You're sure he isn't at home?"

"Quite sure. Are you a friend of his?"

"You could say I'm a connection."

"Well, so far as I know, he's on his way to a place called Mildura."

"Is that right?" He did not sound as if he believed her. "Mind if I come in and see for myself? He's got a way of dodging people sometimes."

It was only then that Rachel noticed that he had his foot inside the door. Suddenly she began to feel frightened of him.

"He isn't here, I tell you," she said.

Her impulse was to slam the door in his face, but with that large foot there it would have been useless.

"Won't take me a moment. I've an appointment with him, see? And I don't feel like having him stand me up."

She could do nothing to stop him as he shouldered his way into the house.

Bungo had retreated a little way, but was still snarling. It did not seem to worry the man.

"Hey, Bungo, old boy, what's got into you?" he said, holding out a hand to the dog. He smiled at Rachel. "He's just putting on a show. He and I are good friends."

Rachel felt a little more confident now that she found the man knew the dog's name.

Once inside the house he did not seem to be in a hurry. He looked round him in a casual way and said, "Been here long?"

"Only since this morning," Rachel replied.

She had a feeling that it might be a good thing to leave the door standing open, but he closed it firmly.

"And where d'you come from?" he asked.

"From London."

"Is that right? Then you'll be feeling pretty tired. Long journey."

"Yes, very long."

"And your brother's out and the Constoupolises have gone to Mildura. Hard on you." There was something mocking in his tone and she became more convinced than before that he did not believe her. "What would they be doing in Mildura, d'you suppose?"

"I don't know. I don't know anything about it." Her voice began to rise. At the same moment the music that seemed to be battering at her brain stopped abruptly and the enormous voice began another incomprehensible speech. "Whatever is that row?" she demanded.

"Pop festival," he answered. "Always have something of the sort here at the Australia Day weekend. You should go out and have a look at what's going on. Huge crowds. Half Adelaide comes out here to listen, or that's what it looks like. But perhaps you don't care for crowds."

"Not much."

"Thought you wouldn't, somehow, by the look of you. I quite like them myself. I like watching people. Has your brother gone to Mildura too?"

"No."

"Sure about that?"

"Yes," she said.

Actually she was not quite sure. She was not quite sure about anything. But the Constoupolises seemed to have been as puzzled by Ian's absence as she was herself, so it seemed unlikely, apart from all the other reasons against his having gone with them, that he might have done so.

The man who called himself Slattery strolled into the sitting-room. She had become less frightened of him now. He repelled her by his heavy grossness and the tinge of mocking impudence in all he said, but she did not feel that he meant any harm to her.

"You can see no one's here," she said, "or do you want to look behind the curtains and under the sofa?"

His mouth was small and only twitched a little when he smiled.

"I'd just like to know, all the same, why you think they've gone to Mildura," he said.

"They left me a message."

"A written message?"

"Yes."

"They didn't just tell you they were going? Why was that?"

"I happened to be in bed and sound asleep when they left and I imagine they didn't want to disturb me. As you said yourself, it was a long journey from London and there's ten hours' difference between the time there and here. All I wanted to do when I got here was to sleep."

"I guess it probably was. How about showing me that message?"

"Look," she exclaimed, "I don't know anything about you. I don't know why you want the Constoupolises or why you pushed your way into the house. I didn't like that. I would like you to leave, only if I ask you to go I don't suppose you'll take any notice of it. But the message was addressed to me and I don't see why I should show it to you."

"Fair enough. But was there something in it you'd really not like me to see?"

The truth was that there was not. It did not matter who saw the message. But to allow him to read it would feel like giving in to him, almost like admitting his right to be in the house. Of course, there was just a possibility that he had a right to be there. He was obviously familiar with it. If only he had not forced his way in and had been readier to explain his relationship with the Greek couple, she would have had nothing against showing him the note that Alex had left behind.

Suddenly he seemed to become impatient, turned and strode out into the passage. The next room into which he looked was the Constoupolises' bedroom. At the sight of the disorder in it he gave a little whistle.

"Looks as if someone left in a hurry," he said.

Rachel stood at his elbow, looking in. She had not given much thought to the state of the room since she had looked into it during her swift search through the house after first waking up, but now she admitted to herself that that was what it looked like.

"If they'd decided to catch an earlier plane than the one they first meant to go on, perhaps they had to hurry," she said.

"So they went by plane, did they, not by car?" He advanced into the room, went to a cupboard and started looking through the clothes hanging inside it. "Now that's funny," he said.

"What is?"

"Never mind. Just a stray thought passing through my head. Now let's look in the other rooms."

She stood in the doorway, barring his way out.

"Will you please tell me what you're doing here," she said. "I'm a stranger. For all I know it's quite all right for you to push your way into the Constoupolises' house and paw about among their belongings, but it looks very peculiar to me."

"Even if it does, there's nothing much you can do about it, is there?" he answered with another of his undersized little grins. "But you needn't worry. I just need to see Constoupolis."

"I've told you, he isn't here."

"And I'm just making sure of that. Not doing any harm, am I?"

He shouldered her out of the way and went into the room that she was occupying.

He had nothing to say about it and next went into Ian's room and then the shower-room. As he went, presumably becoming convinced that Alex and Maria were really not in the house, a heavy frown settled on his face and Rachel suddenly found herself feeling frightened of him again. She wondered what he was likely to do once he was sure that there was no one but herself in the house.

The last room that he went into was the kitchen and there he immediately saw the note from Alex that Rachel had left on the table beside the bottle of wine. He picked it up and read it.

"So you really aren't sure when your brother will be back," he said.

"No, it might be anytime."

"Or not at all."

"What do you mean by that?" she asked sharply.

"Nothing, nothing. No need to get excited."

"Just another thought passing through your head?"

"You might say so. You're worried about him, aren't you?"

He had laid the message down on the table again. Rachel noticed that he had very big hands with thick, square-tipped fingers and an unusual amount of hair on the backs of them. She was sensitive to people's hands and found these particularly repellent.

When she did not answer he suddenly shouted at her, *"Aren't you?"*

"Well, yes, he was supposed to meet me at the airport, but he wasn't there," she admitted. "It isn't like him. Do you know him?"

"Only to say hallo to," he replied quite quietly, as if he had got from her what he wanted. "We've never really got acquainted."

"I think he must have been sent out of town on a job and for some reason hasn't been able to get back yet. I'm wondering if he's been in an accident. If he doesn't come in soon and doesn't telephone, I think I'll ring the police."

"Sounds sensible. Of course you don't know when he went missing."

"I believe he went off to work as usual yesterday morning, then didn't come back at the usual time. That was all the Constoupolises seemed to know about him."

"And that's all you know yourself."

"Haven't I told you so?"

"That's right, you told me. Well, I'll be pushing off. Sorry if I've disturbed you, but I'd this appointment. It's kind of important and I had to be sure . . . No need to go into explanations, is there? I hope you have a happy visit in Australia."

He strode to the front door and let himself out.

A happy visit, Rachel was feeling, to go by her first day here, was something that she might well not have. But when she returned to the sitting-room and sat down Bungo came and tried to climb onto her lap, and even though his bulk was a good deal more than she could accommodate, she felt comforted. He looked offended when she thrust him down onto the rug at her feet, but decided to forgive her and laid his heavy head on her knee, expecting at least to be fondled.

She obliged him while trying to make up her mind what to do. Should she see if it was true that Eudora Linley had no telephone number? Might the Constoupolises have lied to her about that, for some reason not wanting her to get in touch with Eudora? She could not think why they might have done so, but the visit of the man who said he was called Slattery had left a sense behind that the two Greeks might not be all that they seemed. That problem was easily settled, however. She had only to look in the directory.

There was no E. Linley. So there had been no bewildering deception about that.

But as she was turning over the pages of the directory a thought occurred to her which made her start turning

them deliberately, looking for an A. Wellman. She knew
that it would be useless to ring the office where Ian
worked, since on a Saturday afternoon and a holiday at
that it was certain to be closed, but if she could find Andrew Wellman's home address she might be able to get
information from him about Ian's whereabouts.

She found a number in a part of Adelaide called Unley
Park and dialled it.

She let the telephone ring for a long time before putting
it down and returning to her chair, discouraged and once
more overcome by a tiredness which she had almost forgotten while her visitor was here. But it was the kind of
tiredness that produces an almost painful restlessness
which makes the thought of lying down, of trying to relax,
seem wholly unappealing. A drink, she thought, was what
she needed. But not a glass of wine. What she needed was
something much stronger.

Living with Aunt Christina, who had been nearly an
alcoholic, Rachel had become well acquainted with the
magical properties of whisky. She wondered if there was
any in the bungalow. Before going to look for it, however,
she stayed where she was for some minutes, absently
scratching Bungo behind the ears and slipping into a nos-
talgic dream about the house in Edinburgh where she had
lived for some years, first when she was a student at the
university and then when she had taken to teaching at a
school in Morningside.

Aunt Christina, who had been her father's elder sister,
had been a lovable but very singular old woman. She had
been a beauty in her youth and even in her eighties had
retained a good deal of her sparkle and charm. She had
been married three times, becoming richer with each
marriage, but also becoming steadily more prejudiced
against the male sex. It was almost as if she had despised
men for being attracted by her. She seemed to regard her

own charm as a kind of con-trick and anyone who was taken in by it as a fool. It had been mainly because Ian was a man, Rachel believed, and not only because she had been the old woman's companion for several years, that she had left nearly all her wealth to Rachel and only a beggarly legacy of a few thousand pounds to Ian.

The situation had embarrassed Rachel and she had written to Ian, suggesting that they might divide their inheritance more equitably. She had been astonished at how large her share had been. Her aunt had never been mean, but on the whole she had lived modestly, with a notable lack of ostentation. However, Ian had replied to Rachel in a mood of what she had taken to be offended pride, saying that he had no need of money and that she certainly earned her share by enduring Aunt Christina's eccentricities for so long.

The truth was that Rachel had loved the old woman, eccentricities and all, and at the moment, lost in a loneliness that seemed to increase minute by minute, she would have given anything to be back in the old house in the New Town, hearing Aunt Christina's rather hoarse voice floating down to her from the bedroom which towards the end she had hardly ever left, demanding that Rachel should come up and join her in a drink.

But there was no point in thinking about that now. Aunt Christina was dead and the house was sold. Rachel got up and went looking for whisky. But she failed to find any. She found several bottles of wine in a cupboard and some cans of beer, but that was all.

By the time she was sure of this, she had had a new thought. It was that the best thing for her to do would be to take the dogs for a walk. She remembered the glimpse of the sea at the end of Bessborough Street that she had had when she arrived at the bungalow and thought that in spite of the crazily magnified music that was still shattering the peace of the afternoon, some sea-breeze and a

stroll along the beach might do her as much good as anything.

Finding the dogs' leashes hanging from a peg in the
kitchen, she called to them, fastened a leash to each of
their collars and let herself out of the house.

CHAPTER 4

The distance to the sea was only a few hundred yards. In a letter that Rachel had had from Ian he had told her that he was moving into lodgings with the Greek couple because he wanted to be near the sea. He was an enthusiastic and strong swimmer. Today it was very calm and only a little frill of surf along its edge caught a glitter of sunshine on its gently moving surface.

The beach was only a narrow strip of sand with a wide border of grass between it and the road and a row of dark, cone-shaped Norfolk Island pines standing at intervals along it. There was less of a crowd where Rachel reached the beach than she had expected. But at some distance along it, where a jetty jutted out into the sea, a seething mass of humanity was packed solid and it seemed to be from the jetty that the music and the huge voice that occasionally interrupted it were coming.

There were some steps leading down from the road to the beach and Rachel was about to go down them, meaning to let the dogs loose there for a run, when she caught sight of a notice beside the steps. It said that dogs were not allowed on the beach between the hours of ten and five-thirty, and even outside those hours only on a leash.

She looked at her watch. It was only a quarter to five. Yet there seemed to be a fair number of dogs on the beach. Some were chasing balls that were being thrown for them, some were walking sedately beside their owners, some were drowsing peacefully in the afternoon sun. Perhaps, she thought, Australians were the sort of people who were not inclined to take much notice of regulations.

She thought of going down the steps, letting the dogs loose and hoping for the best. But on reflection she made her way towards a bench situated between two pine trees and, to the dogs' obvious chagrin, sat down. For it was a little different for her from what it was for the natives. As a foreigner it would be very embarrassing, she thought, to be found breaking the law, even a very small law that everyone else seemed to be breaking. She decided to rest on the bench for a little while, feeling the freshness of the breeze off the sea on her face, and then go back to the bungalow.

She had been sitting there for only a few minutes when another woman came up the steps, strolled to the bench and sat down at the other end of it. She was in a swim-suit and was straight and slender, yet she had white hair and a deeply wrinkled face.

She gazed out to sea and seemed to be taking no interest in Rachel, but presently she said, "Kind of hypnotic, isn't it? The loudness of that noise, I mean. It does something to you. I suppose that's why the young like it. It gets them all worked up inside. But it's bad for them. Bad for their hearing, you know. They'll all be deaf long before they're my age. I'm seventy-four."

Rachel did not feel that it was expected of her to say that she would never have thought it, though in fact it surprised her.

"How long does it go on?" she asked. "Does it go on all night?"

"Heavens, no! It'll be stopping sometime soon, I hope." The woman turned and looked at Rachel. Her eyes, in her lined, tanned face, were an astonishing blue. "Are you a visitor?"

"Yes," Rachel answered.

"Where do you come from?"

"Scotland."

"I kind of thought you did, from the way you speak. How long have you been here?"

"I arrived this morning from London."

"Is that right? Have you got relatives here?"

"A brother."

"That's nice. You're staying with him, I expect. Does he live here in Betty Hill?"

"He's got lodgings here."

"And those are his dogs?"

"Well, no, not exactly. I'm looking after them for a few days—for a friend."

"I was in Scotland once, and England too, but it's years ago, when my husband was still alive. I live here now, up on the seventh floor of that building, with my son. He's a doctor." She nodded at a tall block of flats that overlooked the beach. "Mostly you'll find it very quiet here. It's just the holiday and this pop festival that's brought everyone out of town. Are you staying long?"

"I'm not quite sure." To her surprise, Rachel found that she did not mind the inquisitiveness of this friendly woman as she had that of the man who had come to the bungalow. In fact, she felt a sudden impulse to confide in her, to tell her of the strange situation in which she found herself. But she restrained it, feeling that it would be too complicated to explain. "I'll see how it goes," she said.

"How long has your brother been here?" the woman went on.

"About two years," Rachel replied.

"Is he married?"

"No."

"Has he come to stay, do you think, or will he go home?"

"I don't know. As a matter of fact . . ." She paused. "As a matter of fact, I haven't seen him since I got here. He's—well, he's busy."

The woman gave her a startlingly shrewd look out of her

very blue eyes. "And left you to look after the dogs when you must be very tired. I call that a shame."

"It isn't his fault," Rachel said quickly. "That's to say . . ." Again she stopped.

"Are you fond of dogs?" the woman asked.

"Oh yes."

Almost as if she wanted to distract Rachel from something which she thought was worrying her, the woman went on, "I was watching a dog playing cricket this afternoon down here on the beach. You'll know we're all crazy about cricket. You can't get away from it. The children start playing it from the time they can walk. Well, I was watching some boys playing down by the water. One was batting, one was bowling and one was fielding on this side. And the other side there was a fine black Labrador and when a ball got hit out to sea, would you believe it, he went swimming after it and brought it back to the bowler. He was having a fine time. And then a police car came along the road and an officer went down and told the kids they'd got to get the dog off the beach. Seemed a pity, they were all enjoying themselves so."

"The police . . ." Rachel began.

"Yes?" the woman said.

"Oh, nothing," Rachel replied. "I suppose they have trouble sometimes with a crowd like that." She nodded towards the jetty.

The woman looked as if she knew that that had not been what Rachel had started to say.

"Sometimes," she said. "The kids get high on drugs occasionally and there may be a bit of violence. We've a big drug problem in Australia. But it's all just as likely to go off peacefully. It's nothing for you to worry about."

"I wasn't worrying about that," Rachel said.

"But about something." The woman smiled at her kindly and stood up. Rachel thought again how slim and straight she was, with the body almost of a girl, though her face was so wrinkled. "I hope that brother of yours isn't busy for too long. He oughtn't to leave you all by yourself on your first day. And I hope you have a happy visit in Australia."

She walked away towards the tall block of flats behind them.

Rachel stayed on the bench for only a few minutes longer, then got up and returned to the bungalow. She had a faint hope that Ian might have returned to it while she was gone, and for a moment, as she opened the garden gate, she had a delusion that he was standing at the door of the house, trying to get in. But then she realized that the man whom she saw there was neither Ian nor had any likeness to him. He was a good deal taller than Ian, more heavily built, and had much lighter coloured hair. It had only been her intense desire that he should be Ian that had briefly deceived her.

He turned when he heard her at the gate. He was about Ian's age, which was twenty-seven, but there all resemblance ended. Ian had a narrow, sharp-featured face with an aquiline nose, rather hollow cheeks and intense dark eyes. This young man had a smooth oval face with soft features that looked as if they might have been tenderly moulded into place by not very experienced fingers which had left the job not quite finished. His eyes were a deep grey with an expression of singular gentleness in them. They were striking, very beautiful eyes. His straw-coloured hair was docked across his forehead and curled into the nape of his neck. He was wearing jeans and a not very clean white shirt, but he himself looked clean.

"Are you Rachel?" he asked. His voice was soft and pleasant.

She acknowledged that she was.

"I'm Pete Wellman," he said. "I'm a friend of Ian's. I've rung the bell, but he doesn't seem to be at home."

"Wellman," Rachel said. "Then you must be in the same firm as Ian."

"No, I've never worked in it," he said. "My father's Ian's boss, but I'm a writer. That is, it's what I'm trying to be. Do you know where Ian is? And Alex and Maria? Have they all gone to the festival or something?"

"No, Alex and Maria have left for Mildura and I haven't seen Ian all day," she said. "He didn't come to the airport to meet me. You don't know anything about where he might be, do you?"

He shook his head. "I haven't seen anything of him for a day or two. You mean nobody met you when you arrived? That was hard on you."

"Well, come inside— Oh lord!" She had started to grope inside her handbag, but suddenly withdrew her hand, exclaiming, "I haven't a key! I didn't think of looking for one when I came out. I just slammed the door shut behind me."

He considered the matter for a moment.

"Are all the windows shut?" he asked. "If one of them isn't I could climb in and let you in."

"I don't know, but I think it may be all right after all," she said. "I don't believe the back door's locked. I let Bungo in at it this morning and I can't remember locking it again after doing that. Let's go and see."

"At the worst you could come to a room I've got in town," Pete Wellman said, "and wait there till Ian shows up. Only we'd have to take the dogs, I suppose. Lucky I brought my mother's car."

"Is that it out there?"

There was a cream-coloured Peugeot in the road outside the gate, to which Rachel had paid no attention as she let herself into the garden.

"Yes," he said. "I haven't a car of my own. Living on the dole, you don't have much to spare for such luxuries."

"Is that what you do then, live on the dole?"

"For the present. I like it better than living with my parents. They're all right, but they don't understand about my writing."

"Well, let's go and take a look at this back door."

Fortunately she was right. The back door was unlocked. She opened it and, accompanied by the dogs, led Pete Wellman into the house.

She could have taken him straight to the sitting-room, but passing through the kitchen he caught sight of the card lying beside the bottle of wine and picked it up and read it. He made no comment on it, putting it down again where he had found it, but his eyes were thoughtful.

"Do you want to see Ian about anything special?" Rachel asked as they entered the sitting-room.

"Nothing important," he answered. "It was just an idea Andy and Sara had. They thought he might like to bring you out to Hindmarsh Island, where they're got a house, for the holiday. I told them I didn't think it was a very good idea. As you and Ian hadn't seen each other for a fair time, I thought you'd probably prefer to be on your own together, and anyway that you'd want to rest after the journey. But they wanted me to suggest it, so I came along."

"Who are Andy and Sara?" Rachel asked.

She had gestured to him to sit down and had sat down herself, but he seemed to prefer standing. Observing him as he stood before her, it struck her that he was very well made and that except for something unformed and immature about his face, he was very good-looking.

"They're my parents," he said. "My mum and dad, but I've never called them that. They stay at the house on Hindmarsh Island a good deal of the time in the summer. It's really very attractive and they'll be delighted if you'd like to come, but of course we'll understand it if you'd sooner not."

"Where is Hindmarsh Island?"

"It's in the mouth of the Murray, just before it reaches

the sea. You know, when that man Sturt who explored the Murray got near the end of it he was sure it would open into a great estuary where they could make a splendid harbour. Then he found the way blocked by an island and the wonderful river dwindled to two quite insignificant streams on either side of it that are no use to anybody. But the island itself is really very pleasant. Would you like to come? It's not much over an hour's drive from Adelaide."

"I could give you an answer to that if I'd seen Ian," she said. "But anyway, I've promised to look after the dogs. So I suppose I'd better say no, though it's very nice of your parents to have thought of it. Please thank them from me and explain what the situation is."

"Except that I don't quite understand what it is," he said. "I know Ian intended to meet you. He told me so when I saw him last. We had a drink together a couple of evenings ago."

"And he said nothing about having to go away?"

"No. I suppose actually you're very worried." His gentle grey eyes dwelt on her face with searching seriousness.

"Yes, I am," she said. "I've been thinking of calling the police to find out if he's been in an accident."

"That might be the best thing to do. But perhaps it might be better to wait a little longer. I don't know. It does seem strange, his disappearing at the moment. Shall I call the police for you? Would you like me to do that? Only I'll tell you what I think. I think from the look of you, you could do with a drink. Suppose we have one now and talk the whole thing over. By the way, do you know about Eudora?"

She hesitated and said, "I'm not sure what you mean. Ian's written about her. I don't know how serious it is, but I've a feeling it means a good deal to him, though he hasn't said so openly. She's your father's secretary, isn't she?"

"Yes, and I just wondered if she could tell us anything, because she seems to be the most likely person to be able to let us know what he's been doing, if there hasn't been an accident or anything like that. But now what about a drink?"

"All right. There's a bottle of wine in the kitchen. I'll get it." She started to get up.

He put a hand quickly on her shoulder, pressing her back into her chair.

"You stay there. I'll get it. You look as if you need someone to take care of you."

He turned to the door.

"Pete—"

He paused. "Yes?"

"Have you got Eudora's telephone number?"

"Yes. Why? Do you want to ring her now?"

"Let's have that drink first, then I'll ring her."

"Right. But perhaps I'd better warn you . . ."

"Well?"

"Oh, it's nothing, but I'm not sure how you'll get on together. You seem to me very different sorts of people."

"Perhaps that means we'll get on very well. One doesn't only make friends with people who are like one, does one? I think most of my friends are quite different from me."

"Yes, I suppose you're right. And, of course, I don't know anything about you yet, do I? I may have got quite a wrong idea about you. Now I'll get that wine."

He went out.

Rachel settled back in her chair and all at once became aware that the tremendous noise coming from outside had stopped. After hearing it going on and on all day the silence seemed almost uncanny. It felt tense and abnormal. The lull before a storm. A quiet that meant that something or other was about to explode.

But that was just foolish. All that the silence meant was that the pop festival was over. She leant back in her chair, briefly allowing her eyes to close.

A moment later Pete was back in the room with the

bottle of wine and two glasses. He put them down on a rickety-looking little coffee-table and poured out the wine. It looked like a claret, but there was an Australian label on the bottle.

"Thank you, Pete," she said. "You're being very kind to me."

"You're welcome." He handed her one of the glasses. "When you've drunk that we'll ring up Eudora, though I think there's a chance she may have gone to Hindmarsh Island already. I know she's spending the holiday there with my family. I hope you'll like her. She thinks I'm idle, which is far from the truth, I work very hard, but I don't think she cares much for me."

He sat down in a chair facing Rachel and sipped his own wine.

She found the flavour of it strange and was not sure that she liked it, but Ian had written to her about the excellence of Australian wine, so perhaps, she thought, it was only a matter of getting used to it. At any rate, its effect was soothing.

They were silent for a little while, Pete watching her in a way which struck her as penetrating as well as kindly. She began to wonder if there really was something immature about his face, or if, for what she guessed was his age, it was unusually, subtly developed.

After a short time he said, "What about calling Eudora?"

"You said you know her number," Rachel said.

"Yes, I'll get it for you, if you like."

He went to the telephone and dialled. After a moment he held it out to her.

"It's ringing," he said.

She rose quickly, took the telephone from him and held it to her ear.

After two or three rings a voice said, "Eudora Linley here."

It was a high-pitched voice, but pleasant.

"I'm Rachel Gairdner," Rachel said. "The sister of Ian Gairdner. I believe you know him."

"Somewhat," the voice said. "Well?"

"I'm sorry to trouble you," Rachel went on, "but I know you're friends and I wondered if by any chance you know where he is. He was to have been at the airport to meet me this morning, but he wasn't there, and he hasn't come back to his lodgings since. If by any chance you know where he is—"

"I don't," the voice interrupted. "We were to have had dinner together yesterday evening, but he stood me up. That's something I don't go for." There was a slight pause, then the quality of the voice changed. It dropped in pitch and became softer. "Look, is something wrong? I mean, if he wasn't at the airport, that's strange. He told me he was going to meet you."

"Could you tell me when you last saw him?" Rachel asked.

"Yesterday morning. He came into the office as usual and we arranged to have dinner together in the evening. I gathered it was going to be—well, a bit of a special occasion. I thought there was something he wanted to be able to tell you when you got here this morning. Not that I'm sure about it. It was just a sort of feeling I had. Then he went out and didn't come back in the afternoon and didn't show up for dinner, though I waited for him in the restaurant, believe it or not, for three-quarters of an hour. And in case it means anything to you, his car's still in the car-park here."

"I hadn't thought about what had happened to his car," Rachel said. "It doesn't sound as if he'd been sent away from Adelaide to do some job or other, does it? That's one of the possibilities I thought of."

"I'm sure he wasn't. I'd have known about it if he had been. Anyway, if for some reason like that he hadn't been able to make it to our dinner, he'd have told me, wouldn't he? Look, where are you now? At Bessborough Street?"

"Yes."

"Suppose I come round to see you. It won't take me long to get there."

"I'd be very grateful if you would. We could talk over what we ought to do."

"Right. I'll be along in about twenty minutes."

Eudora rang off. Rachel also put down the telephone she was holding and turned to Pete. She told him what the other girl had said and that she was coming to the bunga-low. He finished his wine, offered a refill to Rachel and when she shook her head, filled his own glass again, drink-ing it standing.

"I think I'll leave you and Eudora to meet on your own," he said. "You'll probably do better without me. But I'll leave you my telephone number in case you want me. Let me know if there's anything I can do. Have you got a pencil?"

Rachel had a ball-point in her handbag. He wrote a number on a piece of paper he found in a pocket. She put it into her handbag and went with him to the front door. Just before he went out he put a hand on her shoulder and took her by surprise by kissing her gently on the cheek.

"Don't look so miserable," he said. "I'm sure there's some quite simple explanation of everything."

The dogs would have followed him out if Rachel had not caught them by their collars and pulled them back. Get-ting into the car in the road, he drove away.

Returning to the sitting-room, Rachel sat down in the same chair as before to wait for Eudora. She hoped with a touch of desperation that she was going to like her. Ian was her only living relative and during the last two years, when he had been in Australia, she had come to realize how important he was to her. Their father, who had been very much older than their mother, had died of a stroke when Rachel was ten and her mother had soon married again, a solicitor whom Rachel had been unable to like. For a time she and Ian had lived in London and she supposed that really her stepfather had tried to do his best by his wife's children, but he had been a dour, withdrawn man who could not control his jealousy of her love for them, and she and Ian had come to rely very much on one another for affection. Then their mother and stepfather had been killed in a car crash and that was when Aunt Christina had come into the picture.

Thoughts of the old days, of Ian and of what a blow it would be if he had fallen in love with a girl for whom Rachel could feel no liking drifted through her mind as she waited for Eudora's arrival. A dreaminess possessed her. Pictures began to form in her mind of what Eudora would look like and then these imaginary pictures began to develop a bewildering reality, as if the unknown girl was there in the room with her. Rachel's head felt heavy and her eyelids closed. The pictures faded and darkness settled in.

Some time before the twenty minutes were up that Eudora had said it would take her to reach the bungalow in Betty Hill, Rachel had sunk into deep unconsciousness.

CHAPTER 5

The first thing that penetrated that unconsciousness was an enormous voice.

"It's all right, she's coming round."

What was strange about the voice was that it seemed to be in the room. But while Rachel was trying to understand this, she slipped away again into insensibility.

When she woke again it was with a sense of being drowsy and stupid, but no longer in a dream. How long it had been since her first glimpse of the living world she could not guess.

"That's better," the same voice said, but it was no longer enormous. It seemed to come from somewhere close to her ear and was a quiet, pleasant voice.

She opened her eyes. It was a great effort, the lids felt so heavy, but she managed it. The first thing that was in her line of vision was the window.

"It's dark," she protested.

"What can you expect, it's four o'clock," the voice said.

"No," she said, "it was at least five or half past five when I got in, long past four."

"Four o'clock in the morning," the voice explained. "You've been out for several hours. Silly girl. Didn't you know how dangerous it was to do what you did?"

She turned her head a little way, dimly surprised to find it was on a pillow and not leaning against the back of the chair where she remembered that she had gone to sleep. It was also surprising to find that she was in bed and moreover was in a night-dress.

Resisting the desire to let her eyes close again, she looked round. She was in her bedroom and a tall man was standing beside her bed.

"Who are you?" she asked.

"A doctor, luckily for you," he answered.

"But what happened?"

"Can't you remember?"

"I remember I was waiting for someone. Let me think, who was it? I know, it was Eudora, my brother's girl-friend. And I must have dropped off to sleep, I was so tired. But why are you here? Was I taken ill or something?"

"I don't think it would do you much harm to have some coffee," he said. "That might help you to remember a bit more." He raised his voice. For a shuddering moment Rachel thought it was going to be the grossly magnified voice again, making everything unreal, but it was only a call. "How's the coffee coming along, Mother?"

"Ready in a moment," a voice from the direction of the kitchen replied.

The voice seemed vaguely familiar to Rachel, but she could not think why it should be. She kept her attention on the man. He seemed to her to be about the middle thirties and standing over her as she lay in the bed he seemed unusually tall. He was built with a slenderness that increased his appearance of height. His face was narrow, with a long, narrow nose and a long chin and dark brown eyes that were fixed with a grim kind of thoughtfulness on Rachel. He had light brown hair which looked uncombed, as if he had come out to her in a great hurry without stopping to think about it, and he was dressed in a dark blue shirt and jeans.

The room felt very hot and she wondered why someone did not open a window and let in some cool air. Then she remembered that she was in Australia and that the air outside might not be cool.

"How are you feeling now?" the man asked.

"Horrible," Rachel answered.

"That should teach you not to try the same thing again. It was really very foolish."

"What am I supposed to have done?"

"You mean you honestly don't know?"

"I told you, I just went to sleep. I was very tired. I'd been in a plane for twenty-four hours and then I was worried because my brother wasn't here, and I just sat down . . . I know, Eudora must have sent for you. Was it Eudora? Did she find me and get worried about me or something?"

"Someone sent for me. You mean you don't remember that?"

"Why should I?"

"You know, this is really very interesting," he said. "I've never had to deal with a case of amnesia like this before. I wonder how long it's going to last. If it *is* amnesia. And if it isn't, how long are you going to keep up the act? How soon will it be before you realize it might be best to put some trust in me? I'm not going to give you away, you know, unless you're more seriously ill than I think you are at present. If you are, I'm afraid I'm going to need advice. I haven't had much experience of psychiatry."

She felt an immense confusion. "I simply don't know what you're talking about," she said.

"Let's see how you feel when you've had some coffee. By the way, your name's Rachel Gairdner, isn't it?"

"Yes. How do you know that?"

"I found your passport in your handbag."

"What's your name?"

"David Rayne. I live just round the corner from here. Now here comes your coffee."

The door opened and a woman came in. Rachel understood at once why her voice had seemed familiar. It was the woman who had sat beside her on the bench in the afternoon when she had taken the dogs out, the woman with the girl's figure and the wise old wrinkled face. She had said, Rachel remembered, that her son was a doctor.

The woman put the tray down on a table by the bed and slid an arm under Rachel's shoulders.

"You'll feel better, sitting up," she said, and helped Rachel to haul herself up against the pillows. "Feeling any better now?"

"I suppose so," Rachel said because she felt it was what the woman wanted her to say, but she was very pale and her big brown eyes had an almost glazed look, as if they were not really taking in anything. In fact, she was not taking in very much; she could not understand why.

"I knew there was something wrong with you this afternoon," the woman said, "but I didn't think you were on the edge of doing something like this." She turned to her son. "I'll leave you now. I'm sure she'd rather confide in you by yourself rather than in the two of us."

"Right," he said, "but I don't know when I'll be home."

She accepted that with a nod, pouring out a cup of coffee for Rachel, then giving her an encouraging pat on the shoulder before going out.

When she had gone the man said, "My mother used to be a nurse. When we got your message we thought she'd better come along with me, and it happened she recognized you as someone she'd had a chat with in the afternoon. She said you'd seemed worried then about your brother."

"What message?" Rachel asked. "What message am I supposed to have sent?"

"Well, perhaps it wasn't you," he said. "I agree it's possible. It just seems likely that it was you. Now drink that coffee, then let's have a quiet talk about things in general. You needn't be afraid of me, you know. There's no law nowadays against what you've done and all I want is to help you."

"But I haven't done anything!"

"All right, let's suppose for the moment you haven't. Just drink your coffee."

Rachel sipped a little of it. It was very strong and comfortingly hot.

"How did I get to bed?" she asked. "I think I was in a chair in the sitting-room when I went to sleep."

"That's where we found you. And my mother and I put you to bed between us. At first we thought it was a case for the hospital, then I recognized the bottle of pills and realized you couldn't have taken many, though perhaps that was a gamble I shouldn't have taken, but it's turned out all right, hasn't it? And I expect you'd sooner be here on your own than in all the coming and going of a hospital ward. And a stomach pump isn't the pleasantest of treatments."

Perhaps it was the effect of the coffee, or perhaps it was simply that Rachel's mind was beginning to clear of itself, but at last she was beginning to make some sense of the situation.

"You know, you talk just as if you think I'd tried to commit suicide," she said. "Whatever has given you that idea?"

"Isn't it what you wanted us to think?"

She gulped some more coffee and with it felt anger beginning to build up inside her. She very seldom became really angry and she did not know what to do with the unfamiliar sensation.

"Now look," she said, "I've never in my life even thought of suicide! Never! I like life. I want to live a long one. I want to live until I'm very old and probably a nuisance to everyone, because I think I'll probably be enjoying myself even then. And I certainly didn't come all the way to Australia just to kill myself. I could have done it much more comfortably at home."

He gave the first smile that she had yet seen on his rather stern face. It was a smile of unexpectedly attractive warmth.

"You know, you're beginning to worry me," he said. He drew a chair up to the bedside and sat down. "But how do you explain this?" He held out to her a sheet of paper with a few lines written on it.

She took it and read what was written there.

Dear Ian—I'm truly sorry about this but I can't face going on. I can't face the loneliness. I thought when Hamish left me you might be able to help me, but now I hear you're going to be married and you won't want me around. Forgive me if you can. I don't want to make a lot of trouble for you. I hope you and Eudora will be very happy. All my love and goodbye—Rachel.

She stared at the paper with complete disbelief. Then an icy feeling of fear began to creep through her veins.

The man was watching her intently.

"Is that your writing?" he asked.

The lines began to swim before her eyes. She could not focus on them. "Yes—yes, it is. No, it isn't! I didn't write it!" Her voice was shaking and she could hear a shrill note of hysteria in it. "Please, can't you explain it to me? I didn't write it."

"Are you sure we shouldn't assume that you did write it and that because of the pills you took and the state of shock you're in, you can't remember it?"

"No. No, I know I didn't write it. For one thing, it's nonsense about Hamish."

"Who's Hamish?"

She tried to steady the trembling of the hand that was holding the sheet of paper.

"You do seem to want to know an awful lot of things," she said.

"Naturally," he said. "I want to help you."

"Well, Hamish was someone I knew—rather well—but it didn't work out."

"He left you?"

"If anything, I left him, but really we both wanted to put an end to it. He was offered a job in Saudi Arabia and he wanted to take it and I didn't want to go, and so that was that."

"And is that by any chance on your conscience?"

"Oh, for God's sake!" she exclaimed. "Don't go all psychological on me. We parted friends and he sends me a picture postcard from time to time. I've no feelings of guilt about him whatever."

"Who knew of his existence in your life?"

That checked what she had been about to say. It had been to ask him once more about the pills that he seemed to think that she had taken. But at his question she shrank into silence.

"I suppose you think your brother did," he said after a moment.

"Yes," she admitted.

"Did you and he write much to one another?"

"A good deal."

"And tell each other intimate things?"

"Oh yes."

"So he'd have known about Hamish. And without my going what you call all psychological on you, isn't it reasonable for us to think that this affair of yours that broke down, but which you'd told your brother all about, is more on your mind than you want to acknowledge to yourself?"

"No, no, no!" She let the paper fall out of her fingers and pounded the quilt that covered her with both fists. "It may look a bit like my writing, but I didn't write it."

"You mean it's a forgery?"

"It must be."

"By someone who knew all about Hamish?"

"I suppose so. I don't know. I can't make any sense of it. Now tell me about the pills."

He took up a small bottle from the table beside her bed and held it out to her. It was empty.

"It's some stuff called Somnolin," he said. "I've been prescribing it for some time for Maria Constoupolis, who happens to be a patient of mine. It's a sleeping-pill and it's fairly potent, but I never gave her more than a few at a time. And even if the bottle had been full, I don't believe it would have finished you off. The question is, did you know that or didn't you?"

She gave him another long stare, then managed a dry little laugh.

"I think I'm beginning to understand," she said. "You don't think I tried to commit suicide at all. You think I faked all this to get some attention for somebody. I've been left by my lover, I come to Australia to try to forget it, my brother lets me down and doesn't trouble to meet me, I feel ill used and neglected and I fake this whole thing to get someone, anyone—as it happens, you—to come and listen to me talk about my woes and look after me. And that brings me to a question I'd like to ask you. Why did you come here? You don't drop in on most of your patients at four o'clock in the morning on the off chance that they may be feeling suicidal, do you?"

"No, it wasn't quite like that, though I admit it was a little peculiar." His long face was grave. He had picked up the sheet of paper that was lying on the bed and looked at it with a puzzled frown. "At a bit before four o'clock I had a telephone call. A voice said, 'There's a woman dying at 21 Bessborough Street.' And that was all. Whoever it was rang off. I was half inclined to treat it as a practical joke because there'd been that pop affair yesterday and I thought there might be drunks and just troublesome fools roaming the streets. But someone had my number and knew I was a doctor and anyway I couldn't take the risk that it was only a gag, so I got up and dressed and that happened to wake my mother and I told her what had happened and she insisted on coming with me so that I'd have a witness in case it turned out to be something really nasty. A murder, for instance. That thought did cross my mind."

"And all you found was a fake suicide. How disappointing for you."

He did not respond to the sarcasm in her voice except that his frown deepened a little.

"Suppose we accept that what you say is true," he said, "and that you didn't knowingly take the pills and write the letter; what's your explanation of what really happened?"

She closed her eyes for a moment, trying to think. But as soon as she did that her thoughts once more became lost in confusion.

Opening her eyes again and looking into his face, which with the frown on it looked disturbingly severe, as if he had made up his mind in advance that she was about to lie to him, she said, "I wish I didn't feel in such a muddle. I can't think properly. Is it the drug? Tell me, was it a man's voice or a woman's that you heard on the telephone?"

"I'm not sure," he said. "It was over so quickly I couldn't really tell. It was rather high-pitched, so I thought it was a woman's, but it might have been a man's if he was speaking falsetto to disguise it. Does that mean anything to you?"

"No. But how did you get into the house?"

"By the back door. It was unlocked."

"Oh yes, of course. But what about the dogs? Didn't they bark at you?"

"Yes, but you were still too deep under to be disturbed by them. Then they got used to us and by now I think they're both sound asleep in the kitchen."

"Useful watch-dogs! You know, if it was a murder that didn't come off . . ." She paused.

"Yes?" he said.

"You did say, suppose I didn't take the pills *knowingly,* didn't you?"

"Yes."

"That would mean that someone gave them to me."

"Of course."

"And that could only have been Pete Wellman, though why he should have done such a thing I can't imagine."

"Pete *Wellman?*" he said in a startled tone.

"Yes. Do you know him?"

"I know the whole family fairly well. I used to be in practice in Adelaide before I moved out to Betty Hill and Mrs. Wellman was my patient. But what would Pete have been doing in this house at four in the morning, because whoever rang me up must have been in here and seen the empty bottle and your letter?"

"Not my letter!"

"All right, we'll leave it at that for the moment. But why do you think it was Pete who gave you the poison?"

"Because we had a drink together out of a bottle of wine the Constoupolises left for me in the kitchen. I was asleep when they left for Mildura, you see. But the only thing I had to eat or drink since I got here, except for some coffee I had with Alex and Maria soon after I arrived, was the wine. And if the pills had been in the coffee Maria gave me they'd have acted much sooner than they did, wouldn't they?"

"Oh yes, they act quite fast. But let me get this straight. There was a bottle of wine in the kitchen that the Constoupolises left for you when they went away?"

"Yes."

"Did they pull the cork for you?"

"Yes."

"And you and Pete had drinks together out of it?"

"Yes, and I thought it tasted a bit strange, but I thought that was only because I'm not used to Australian wine. And it was Pete who fetched it from the kitchen and poured it out and gave it to me, and actually he had two glasses of it while I had just the one—"

"Wait! Wait a minute!" He sprang to his feet. "You say

that bottle was standing in the kitchen with its cork drawn for you don't know how long, so someone—anyone—could have got at it and put the drug into it long before Pete got there. You were asleep in the morning, you say, and wouldn't have known anything about it. And if Pete had two glasses of the stuff he may be in a much worse state than you. I'm going to telephone him now. Do you know his number?"

"You'll find it in my handbag, and you know where that is if you looked for my passport in it."

"Right. Then wait a minute. I've got to see if I can get through to him. If I can't I'll have to leave you to yourself, since you're over the worst of it, and drive in and see what's happened to him."

A long, lean figure, tense with a new anxiety, he shot out of the room.

CHAPTER 6

After a short pause Rachel heard the tinkle of the telephone bell as he lifted it, then there was a longish silence before he began to talk. When she heard the sound of his voice she could not distinguish what he said, but if it was not to Pete that he was talking, he had got through to someone. Someone who perhaps might not be in a very good temper at being wakened at four in the morning.

Vaguely listening, she tried to concentrate on one question among all the others that were crowding into her mind. For whom had the drugged wine been intended?

The bottle with its cork drawn had stood on the kitchen table for most of the day and she had left the back door unlocked after letting in the dogs. So anyone could have got in and doped the wine while she was down by the sea, having left the house empty, and in that case the poison might have been meant for Alex or Maria by someone who did not know that they had gone away. For all she knew, they might have any number of enemies who would be glad to speed them out of the world.

But Alex had left his note to Rachel beside the winebottle, so anyone who had come in, seen the bottle and thought that here was a splendid opportunity for committing murder would have known that Alex and Maria had left already for Mildura. It would not be they who drank the doctored wine.

But it might have been Ian.

It was at that moment that Rachel remembered the man who had said his name was Slattery.

It seemed to her that he would not be a very nice man to have among one's acquaintances. Not nice at all. She found it quite easy to imagine him poisoning a bottle of wine. And she thought it quite probable that although he had looked through the house for the two Greeks and failed to find them, he had not really believed that they had gone away, but might have thought that they would return later and drink the wine. And if it happened that an extra victim, for instance the unhelpful girl from England, suffered the consequences with them, what did it matter? Besides poisoning a bottle of wine, Rachel was in a mood to think, it was even easy to imagine that this was not his first murder, that there had already been a number of unfortunate people who owed an early death to him.

But she was not really convinced by this line of reasoning. There were several things the matter with it. It was true that the man could have got into the house while she had been out with the dogs, but he could not have forged this extraordinary letter.

Whoever had done it had not only been able roughly to imitate her writing, but had known about Hamish. And that could not be Mr. Slattery. Ian was a fairly reticent person and if he had confided in anyone about the matter, it would not have been that gross bully of a man.

David Rayne came back into the room.

"It's all right, he's vomited the stuff up," he said. "He's been sick a number of times, he said. It affects some people that way if they take an overdose. He's feeling very sorry for himself, but it's the best thing that could have happened."

"It was Pete himself you were talking to, was it?" Rachel said.

"Yes. And now the question is, what are we going to do about you?"

"You needn't do anything."

He sat down again on the chair by the bedside.

"You do worry me, you know, you really do," he said. "You don't *seem* like a girl who'd do a damn fool thing like fake a suicide to attract attention, and you don't seem like a real suicide either. You'd be in a far worse state now than you are if that's what you were. So we've got to consider murder, haven't we?"

"You sound very cheery about it."

"Well, I don't see how what's happened could possibly be accidental. Yet murder doesn't seem to suit you either."

"Thank you."

"Does anyone hate you? Is anyone afraid of you? Tell me, can you think of anyone with a motive for wanting you out of the way?"

"No, I can't," she said, "and I think it would be easiest for you if you made up your mind that, as you just said, I faked this suicide to attract attention. Then you could go home with a good conscience and get some sleep before you have to start your day's work. After all, it fits the circumstances better than anything else. I can see that. I arrive here, I'm in an unstable state of mind because I've recently been abandoned by my boy-friend, then my brother fails to be at the airport to welcome me and seems to have gone off somewhere without troubling to explain why, then his landlady and her husband disappear too and I'm left all alone in this strange country with no one taking an interest in me and no one to turn to. So I begin to feel neglected and desperate and then I find some sleeping-pills somewhere in the house and suddenly it occurs to me how I could get someone round here to bother about me. I'll take the pills and I'll write the suicide note, then I'll telephone a doctor and tell him there's someone dying at this address and trust to luck he'll come. And then I'll have someone to talk to and he'll advise me what to do." She gave a sardonic smile. "Now be honest, that's what you really think, isn't it?"

"Only now I'm here you don't seem to want to talk to

me," he said. "If anything, you seem in rather a hurry to get rid of me."

"Perhaps you aren't what I expected. Perhaps I thought you'd be a kindly old father-figure who'd never have any suspicions of me."

He stroked the side of his sharp chin. "Well, I'll be honest, until a little while ago I was thinking pretty much along the lines you've suggested. But we've got to fit Pete Wellman into the picture, haven't we? You say he was here this afternoon and drank some wine with you. And I understand he started feeling sick fairly soon after he got home. But you didn't phone me, if it was you, until nearly four this morning, which means you couldn't have drunk any of the drugged wine at the same time as he did. The stuff would have worked in about half an hour, if you aren't used to it. Do you normally take any drugs?"

"Just the occasional aspirin."

"So it doesn't seem to fit, does it?"

She stirred restlessly in the bed. "Really I'd like to stop thinking about it. I can't make any sense of it and the more we talk about it, the more confusing it gets."

"Well, there's still another problem we haven't asked ourselves yet. If it was you who telephoned me this morning, how did you get my telephone number?"

"Didn't you say Maria Constoupolis is a patient of yours? She's probably left a note of it somewhere."

"That's true. You're a good devil's advocate when you put your mind to it. Now tell me about this brother of yours. What do you think he's doing?"

"Oh God, that's what I wish I knew!" At that moment she nearly burst into tears. "We're good friends, we always have been, and he wanted me to come out here and stay for a time, and he was going to meet me and he'd have brought me here and I understood from the Constoupolises that he and I were to look after the dogs while they were away, visiting friends. But he's just disappeared and that isn't like him, and I think perhaps I ought to call the police about it. But you know, when you're a stranger in a place you know nothing about, you're afraid of making a fool of yourself . . ." She stopped herself because she heard her voice beginning to rise again with a note of hysteria in it.

He was watching her with the concentration which she had already thought gave his face a kind of grimness, though his smile could make it suddenly kind and warmly friendly.

"Who's Eudora?" he asked abruptly.

"She's Mr. Wellman's secretary," she answered. "And I understand she's Ian's girl-friend. From the way she spoke yesterday I had a feeling they were thinking of getting married."

"You saw her yesterday?"

"No, I only talked to her on the telephone. I got her number from Pete. I thought, you see, she might know something about where Ian had gone. But she didn't seem to know anything. They were to have had dinner together the evening before and he didn't turn up. Naturally, she was rather angry about it, but then she seemed to realize there was something to worry about and she said she'd come round to see me. But before she got here I'd gone to sleep."

"So you don't actually know if she came or not."

"No."

"Perhaps we ought to get in touch with her and find out if she did come round."

"But you can't do that at this hour of the morning!"

He gave a sigh, as if he were getting a little weary of so many problems. His gaze, instead of concentrating on her face, became abstracted. "D'you know, I think I'm going to have some of that coffee of yours. I'll get a cup. Wouldn't you like some more yourself?"

"Yes, please." She held out her cup to him.

He refilled it and went out of the room. After a minute he was back with a cup which he filled from the pot on the table beside her. The same abstracted look was still on his face.

"I just took a look into the lounge," he said. "As I remembered, there's a half-empty bottle of wine there. I think I'll take it away with me. I know one of the forensic people in the university and I could get him to analyse it. I'm sure it was Somnolin in the wine, but he'll be able to tell us about its strength. Because that's one of the things that's puzzling about the present situation. Why, if someone was trying to poison you and leave that letter to make it look like suicide, didn't they make a better job of it and put enough stuff into the wine to make sure of finishing you off? It's true I don't think Maria had enough to do it, but he could have brought some more of his own."

"For God's sake, stop!" she cried and in a momentary excitement spilled some of her coffee on to the sheet that covered her. "D'you think it's nice to lie here thinking that the moment I arrived in Australia someone tried to murder me? You know as well as I do that it simply can't be true. And thinking about it really doesn't help."

"I'm sorry," he said. "Yes, I'm being stupid. Let's talk about what we're going to do. You want to call the police, don't you, about your brother having gone missing?"

"Don't you think it's the only thing to do?"

"Probably it is. Shall I do it for you now?"

"Isn't it too early in the morning?"

"I think they supply a twenty-four-hour service."

"But won't they think it very strange that I waited until about half past four to call them when I could have done it any time yesterday?"

"I expect they're used to much stranger things than that. For one thing, they'll know that people's nerves have a way of cracking in the early morning, after a sleepless night."

"Mine wasn't sleepless, was it? And won't I have to explain that? And what you're doing here?"

"You don't want to do that?"

"I don't know. No, I don't think I want to tell them about this suicide business. They're going to think just what you did. Perhaps what you really still think, though you don't feel that admitting it is the best sort of treatment to give me. Because who could have forged this letter and planted it beside me? I can understand what absolute nonsense that seems, so I don't want to have to talk to strange policemen about it. I think I'd sooner wait until a bit later, say half past seven or eight o'clock, and then ring them up and tell them about how worried I am about my brother not having come home. Then I needn't say anything about the letter, or the wine, or the mysterious suicide that didn't come off."

"Yet those are just the things that we need to know about."

She noticed that he included himself in this need for knowledge. There was something reassuring about it.

"Really what I want to know is simply what's happened to Ian," she said. "I've a feeling that if we knew that, all the other things would unravel themselves or perhaps turn out to be simply unimportant. And I do think you ought to go home and have some rest before your day's work begins. Don't you have to be at a surgery or something sometime in the morning?"

"Not today. It's Sunday. And it's all right, I'm used to having my sleep interrupted. And if it happens that I'm wanted badly somewhere, my mother will take the call and phone through to me here. You see, the fact is, I don't like leaving you alone until we've got the police here. Someone's bungled once, but suppose they do something more drastic another time."

"Dr. Rayne, I believe you *enjoy* frightening me!" Then at something she saw in his face, which might actually have been a trace of hurt, she added quickly, "But it's very good of you to worry. If I'd been called out about a crazy thing like this, I'm sure I shouldn't be so tolerant. But do please go home."

He stood up and for a moment she thought that he was going to do as she urged and at once she felt a surge of fear that he was going to leave her. But all he did was help himself to more coffee.

"I think the best thing to do, since you don't want to call the police yet, is to try to get some sleep," he said. "Some normal sleep. And I'll go and have a lie-down on that quite comfortable-looking sofa in the lounge, and presently I'll get some breakfast. Then I'll phone the Triple O. I don't suppose you know what that is."

She shook her head.

"It's the same as your 999. I'll report a missing person. Now remember, I'm only in the other room, if you want me. Sleep well."

Taking his cup with him, he left the room, switching the light off as he went.

Rachel heard him go to the sitting-room, but did not hear him close its door. He had deliberately left it open, she thought, so that he would hear it if she were to get up and start doing anything strange, like going to the shower-room and helping herself to some of the other pills that were there. Or he might just conceivably be afraid that someone else would come back into the house to finish off what he had so far failed to accomplish.

Lying still in the darkness, she did not feel in the least like going to sleep. She had had enough sleep for the time being. Wakeful and restless, she wondered how serious the earnest young doctor had been in talking as if he thought that someone might really have tried to murder her.

It was not as if some maniac had got into the house, attacked her, raped her, robbed her, or done any of the things that needed no rational motive, though she supposed that the percentage of such people in the population of Australia was as high as anywhere else. What had happened was complex and must have been carefully thought out. The forgery of the letter alone must have taken a fair amount of trouble.

She was on the edge of sleep by now, with a dreamy feeling that in trying to solve the puzzle of what had happened the day before she had forgotten something and that it was something important. When anything of that kind happened, she knew, the best thing to do was to stop thinking about the problem, then the memory would suddenly return of itself. In any case, her thoughts were no longer making sense. She seemed to be in an aeroplane in which an enormous voice, a voice of such intolerable volume that it beat on her ear-drums with the pain that she always felt in an aeroplane when it started to descend, announced, "Ladies and gentlemen, we are about to crash. Please keep your seat-belts fastened and do not panic. It will be a first-class crash. Everything has been arranged for your comfort. Now dilly, dilly, dilly ducks, come and be killed, For you must be stuffed and my customers be filled . . ."

Then came the crash, only it seemed surprisingly soft and gentle and she woke up, realizing that she had been asleep for a considerable time.

It was Bungo, the boxer, who seemed to have taken a fancy to her, who wakened her by jumping on to her bed and nuzzling her face. The door was open and Charlie, the little brown dog, a more detached character, was in the doorway, looking around curiously, as if things in the room were not quite as he expected.

Then David Rayne appeared, carrying a tray. He had made tea and a considerable quantity of toast and apparently had found butter and marmalade in the kitchen.

"It's a quarter past seven," he said. "I thought it was about time to get active."

"Have you been on that sofa in the sitting-room all night?" she asked.

"There wasn't much of the night left."

"Did you get any sleep at all?"

"Off and on. It's all right, I told you, I'm used to it. But I've thought of something. You told me that yesterday afternoon you phoned a girl called Eudora and that she said she was going to come and see you, but you went to sleep before she got here. Well, suppose you phone her now before you call the police and ask her if she came, and if so, did she notice anything unusual."

"Only I haven't got her number," Rachel said.

"Then how did you get through to her yesterday?"

"Pete did it. He dialled the number, then as soon as it began to ring, he handed the phone to me."

"I'll phone him then and ask for the number. You get on with your breakfast."

He planted the tray on her knees and went out.

As Rachel began on the toast and marmalade it occurred to her that this was the first solid food that she had eaten since leaving the aeroplane. She ate all the toast that the doctor had made and would not have minded some more.

When he returned from the sitting-room, she said, "Do all your patients get this sort of treatment?"

He sat down and watched with approval the sight of her appetite.

"Normally they don't require it," he answered. "The problems they present me with may be life-and-death matters and far more distressing than yours, but they're basically less intriguing."

"Did you get Eudora's number?"

"Yes, here it is." He had written it down on a scrap of paper. "I had a few words with Pete. He seems to have recovered. He says he may come in to see you later in the day."

"Then if you'll leave me while I have a shower and get dressed," she said, "I'll phone Eudora."

"And the police," he reminded her.

"I thought you said you'd do that."

"That was last night. I didn't think you were up to it. But wouldn't it be best for you to do it? In fact, if you don't want to tell them about the suicide, attempted murder or whatever it was, the sooner I get out of the way the better. Are you sure you don't mean to tell them about all that?"

"Quite sure."

"I think you're making a mistake."

"It's possible."

But there was something that was not possible. It was to tell this singularly kind and understanding man, and after that some policeman who for all she knew might be neither kind nor understanding, that she could think of only one person who, if you did not know him, might conceivably have some motive for murdering her, and that was Ian.

CHAPTER 7

Rachel's talk on the telephone with Eudora was unsatisfactory. It told her nothing. First, Eudora was annoyed at being called so early, and when she was annoyed, it appeared, her rather high-pitched voice went shrill. When Rachel asked her if she had seen or heard anything of Ian since their talk the afternoon before, Eudora became indignant.

"You're asking me if he spent the night here, are you?" she said. "What do you take me for?"

Rachel did not think it impossible that Ian had spent the night with her, but she answered quietly, "I wasn't thinking of anything like that. I simply thought that you might have seen him yesterday evening, or heard from him, or heard something about him. I'm very worried about the way he's disappeared."

"Well, I don't know a thing," Eudora said. "And where were you when I came to see you?"

"You came, did you?"

"Of course I came. I said I would, didn't I?"

"Yes. Yes, well, I—" Rachel did not know how to explain what had happened without saying more than she intended. "To tell you the truth, I fell asleep. I'm very sorry. It was the journey, I think, and trying to make that switch of ten hours around the clock. I simply didn't know where I was yesterday. I'm only just beginning to get adjusted. You rang the bell, did you?"

"I rang the bell and I knocked and nobody answered, so I went away."

"You didn't think of seeing if the back door was open?"

"Now why should I do that? If I come visiting someone and they don't choose to let me in, I don't normally go prowling round the house to see if I can get in by the back door or a window."

"No, of course not. I'm sorry, I know I'm not being very sensible, but I'm so worried about Ian. I'm just going to call the police about him."

There was a slight pause, then with the shrillness gone from her voice, Eudora said, "Perhaps that would be the best thing to do. And I'm sorry you're so worried. I'm worried too, of course, but I thought for sure he must have gone home yesterday evening. In fact, I thought it was why you didn't answer the door when I rang. I thought you'd probably gone out together for a meal, and meeting each other after all this time, had simply forgotten me. I'm only just beginning to take it in that he's still missing. What would you like me to do? Shall I come round to see you? I was going out to Hindmarsh Island. The Wellmans have a house down there by the Murray and they invited me for the week-end, but I could cancel that."

"I shouldn't do that," Rachel said, liking the girl better now. "If you're needed for some reason, I suppose I could get in touch with you."

"You can telephone. Have you a pencil handy? I can give you the Wellmans' number."

Rachel took the ball-point pen from her handbag and made a note of the number that Eudora gave her.

Eudora went on, "But isn't there anything I can do? I mean, I'm beginning to understand how worried you must be. As I said, if it would help at all, I'll ring Mr. Wellman and say I've got to call the visit off. It really isn't all that important to me." There was charm in her voice now and sympathy that sounded genuine.

"It's very kind of you, but I'm all right," Rachel answered. "And if I hear anything, I'll let you know."

"Yes, do that. Please do that. It'll be on my mind all day until we know something. What do you think *can* have happened to him? Could he have been kidnapped?"

"Kidnapped?" It was Rachel's voice that was shrill now. "Whoever would do that? Who is there who could pay a ransom?"

"I thought you were awfully rich," Eudora said.

There was something in the way that she said it, simply, almost casually, taking the fact for granted, that gave Rachel a start of panic. For if Eudora could think this, how easily might others think it too. If she, with access to reliable information from Ian, could think it, might not other more ignorant people believe it?

"I don't think I'm what you'd call *awfully* rich," Rachel said. "Only fairly so. Far more so than I ever expected to be and if I've got to pay a ransom I'll do it. I'll talk that over with the police. But I thought when kidnappers took the risk of snatching somebody, they expected to be paid in millions."

"You aren't a millionairess?"

"Certainly not."

"Well, I'm sorry I brought it up," Eudora said. "I don't want to add to your worries. I guess I was just being stupid. What do those Greeks think about what might have happened to him?"

"I don't know," Rachel said. "They've gone away for the week-end. They told me they knew nothing about him."

"You mean you're all alone?"

Rachel glanced over her shoulder to where David Rayne was sitting, listening with interest to her end of the conversation.

"Yes," she said, "I'm alone."

"But you're sure you wouldn't like me to come round? You know, I've always thought there was something a bit sinister about those Greeks. I never liked Ian's living with them."

"Come if you want to," Rachel said, "but I don't think there's anything you can do."

"In that case, then . . ." Eudora sounded on the whole relieved at having been let off the hook. "But mind you let me know if anything happens."

Rachel promised that she would and they both rang off.

David Rayne stood up, stretching his lean body with the first sign of weariness that he had shown.

"So now we've got to think about kidnapping, have we?" he said. "Is that really so fantastic?"

"I don't know what local customs are in the matter," Rachel said.

"Well, I heard you say you're a fairly rich woman. I didn't know that. But if you are, perhaps you shouldn't brush the idea aside too hastily. Would your brother have talked about it to people he knows less about than Eudora? Perhaps boasted about it? Exaggerated it?"

She had put her hand on the telephone again. "I'm sure he'd have done the reverse. I'm surprised he told even Eudora about my legacy. But anyway, why should kidnappers come back and try to poison me and leave a forged suicide letter behind? The one thing they would want to be sure of is that I'm alive and able to sign a cheque. Now I'm going to phone the police."

"Go ahead," he said.

She dialled what he had called the Triple O and after asking for the police and giving the Constoupolises' telephone number and waiting for a while, she found herself connected with someone who said that he was Police Headquarters. He had a courteous, impersonal voice and when she said that she wanted to report a missing person, he asked her to hold on for a moment while he put her through to someone else.

The voice that then spoke was as precise as the other had been, but was a woman's.

She listened to Rachel's hurriedly told story, asking a

question or two, but Rachel could not help feeling that the importance of the worry that she described diminished as she told it. Ian was not a child who had been led away by a stranger. He was not a girl who had probably been raped and strangled and her body dumped in the River Murray. He was unlikely to be a spy who had defected to Russia. He was simply a young man who ought to have known how to take care of himself.

However, the woman took Rachel's name and address and was asking her if she had a photograph of her brother when she suddenly paused.

There was a change in her tone when she went on, and if she had not carefully kept her voice level, Rachel would have said that a new excitement had entered it.

"Please wait a moment," the woman said. "Twenty-one Bessborough Street, you said. I think Sergeant Ross should hear about this."

Sergeant Ross sounded as detached as his colleague and as Rachel repeated her story asked almost identical questions. The only difference was that as soon as he had heard as much as he apparently wanted to know he said that he would be round at the bungalow in about a quarter of an hour.

Rachel supposed that this should have reassured her, but in fact it scared her, for what had there been about giving her name and address which had made the policewoman become particularly interested in her? That she had become interested, and that very suddenly, was something of which Rachel felt sure. But did that mean that the police had information about Ian which might be of some very frightening kind? Had they found him, or at least found his body? Could that be possible? That, or something somehow as terrible? It was very puzzling, because if they already had Ian's name and address and so had had no difficulty in identifying him, why had they not been along to Bessborough Street before now?

Feeling very shaken, she crossed the room and dropped into a chair.

"A Sergeant Ross is coming," she said.

David Rayne said, "Then I'll leave you to cope with him as you think best. But remember, I think you'd be wise to tell him the whole story of what happened last night. It's not for me to do it. In a sense you're my patient and that makes it confidential between us, so unless you call me in again I'll do nothing more about it. I only wish I understood why you want to be so secretive about it."

She gave him a curious look, searching and thoughtful.

"You mean you really don't understand?" she said.

"No."

"Even now that you've heard I'm a rich woman?"

He looked blank for a moment, then his eyebrows shot up in a sudden look of comprehension.

"So that's what you think—that Ian did it! That's why you won't talk about it."

"No, I *don't* think so, but it's what other people are going to think when they hear the story. So I'm not going to tell it."

"I see, I see. Yes, you may be right, then. Well, I'm taking this bottle with me and I'll let you know if my forensic friend has anything of interest to say about it. And I hope you get on well with Sergeant Ross."

He picked up the half-empty bottle, jammed the cork back into its mouth and hurried out.

Ten minutes later Sergeant Ross rang the doorbell.

His arrival was heralded by excited barking from Bungo and Charlie. Rachel had let them both out into the garden as soon as she got up and the first thing she did when she opened the door to the sergeant was to make sure that he had closed the garden gate behind him so that the dogs could not stray into the road. He had done so and had both the dogs at his heels, sniffing and barking at him.

He was in plain clothes, a lightweight grey suit, a grey-

and-white-striped shirt and a dark blue tie. He was a tall man of about forty and at first sight gave a misleading impression of being too lightly built to be strong enough for his kind of employment, but he in fact moved with the elasticity that comes only from powerful and well-coordinated muscles. His hair was a light brown that almost matched the brown of his skin. He had a high forehead and a mouth that was slightly crooked, one corner of which lifted as he greeted Rachel with what looked like a sceptical half-smile, though the expression of his eyes was sombre.

"Miss Gairdner?" he said.

"Yes. Please come in." She felt even more anxious now than she had before his arrival. "Have you anything to tell me about my brother?"

"I'm afraid not," he answered. "I've come to see what you can tell me."

She led him into the sitting-room. She was wishing now that David Rayne had stayed. After all, he and this man were both Australians, might even have met at some time in a city the size of Adelaide and, besides that, were both men. It was odd, in a way, that that last should have occurred to her, for she had never at any time in her life been able to rely much on the protection of men. But at least, she thought, they would have been able to communicate with one another more easily than she would be able to with this stranger. On the other hand, perhaps the truth was simply that she liked having David Rayne there. It was only after he had left that she had realized how much he had supported her.

"You haven't any news of an accident, then," she said, "or anything like that?"

"Nothing at all," he said. His voice was grave and formal but not unfriendly. "But I understand that you're very concerned at his not being here when you arrived. You arrived yesterday, is that right?"

"Yesterday morning," she answered. "He was to have met me at the airport, but he wasn't there, so I came here by taxi, because this was the address he'd given me, and his landlady and her husband were here and they told me he'd gone off to work as usual the morning before, but hadn't come back in the evening and they hadn't seen him since. And I tried not to worry about it for a time, but when I woke up this morning and he still hadn't come back, I thought it might be best to get in touch with the police. If I've done something silly and am just wasting your time, I'm very sorry."

"Not at all. Best thing you could have done. Naturally you're worried." The tilted half-smile remained on his face but had nothing humorous about it. "Has he ever done anything like this before? I mean, at home in Britain. I think you told me he'd been here about two years."

"He's never done anything like it. He's a very responsible sort of person. I can't imagine him disappearing— voluntarily, I mean. I'm sure he must have been in an accident, or—or something like that."

"About this landlord and landlady of his, aren't they here?" he asked.

"No, they left yesterday afternoon—I suppose it was in the afternoon, although I was quite confused about the time of day here. I'm only just beginning to get used to it. They left to visit some friends in a place called Mildura."

"So you're alone."

"Yes."

"And did these Constoupolises say when they'd be back?"

She gave him a puzzled look. She was sure that she had not mentioned the name, either on the telephone or since he had arrived here.

"Do you know them, then?" she asked.

"Oh, we've had some contact," he answered casually. "A driving offence of some sort, I think it was. Failed a breathalyser test, perhaps that was it. I can't remember offhand. But did they say when they'd be back?"

Rachel did not for a moment believe his explanation of how he happened to know that the people who lived in this bungalow were called Constoupolis. If Alex had been arrested for drunken driving it would have been by someone in the uniformed branch, not a detective sergeant. It was interesting, however, and slightly frightening, that Alex and Maria appeared to be "known to the police," if that was the phrase they used for it here.

"I think they'll be back on Monday evening, or perhaps early on Tuesday morning," she said. "And there's another odd thing. My brother had promised to look after their dogs for them while they were away, and it isn't like him simply to forget a thing like that."

"But you're here to do it for him, so the Constoupolises could still go away."

She nodded.

"How did they go? By car?" he asked.

"No, there's something the matter with their car," she said. "They went by plane. And there's something a little odd about that too, though I don't suppose it's important. I went to bed very soon after I got here, you see, and I understood they were going to leave for Mildura early this morning, but when I got up after a time I found they'd gone and they'd left their room in an awful mess, as if they'd changed their minds and decided to go yesterday all of a sudden and had had to hurry to catch a plane. But they'd left some food for me in the fridge and a note to tell me what they'd done."

"I'd like to see the note."

Rachel was beginning to feel that he was more interested in the Greeks than he was in Ian.

"I think it's in the kitchen," she said.

She went out to the kitchen and found the note still on the table. She brought it to the sitting-room and gave it to the detective. He looked at it briefly, then handed it back to her.

"And was there a quiche and all the rest of it in the fridge?" he asked.

"I haven't actually looked." She was glad that he did not ask about the bottle of wine and whether she had managed to drink all of it by herself, and if not, what had happened to the rest of it.

"I'd like to look at this room of theirs," he said.

She took him to the Constoupolises' bedroom and let him go ahead of her into it. For a moment he stood still, just inside the door, as if he were trying to fix a first impression of the disorder there on his memory, then he strolled forward and without touching anything looked thoughtfully at the clothes scattered on the floor and on the bed and at what was left hanging in the wardrobe.

Then, taking his chin in his hand and pulling it absently, he observed, "That's funny."

Rachel felt a prickling sense of shock. That was just what the man called Slattery had said when he had taken a look around the room. The thought of that man still made her feel uneasy.

"What's funny?" she asked.

"Well, if you were going to Mildura at this time of year, would you take all your winter clothes with you and leave such a lot of summer things behind? D'you realize, there isn't a woollen suit, or a skirt, or a sweater, or an overcoat anywhere in the room?"

"I don't know anything about Mildura," she said. "Is it cold there?"

"Being inland, it's a hell of a lot hotter than Adelaide."

"Perhaps then they just got tired of all their winter clothes," she suggested. "That happens to one sometimes. And one hands them over to Oxfam or someone like that and goes in for an orgy of buying new things."

He gave her a long look as if he were trying to decide how serious she was.

She chose that moment to say with sudden violence, "Will you tell me why you want to know so much about these people instead of asking me questions about my brother?"

"Fair enough," he said. "Let's go back to the lounge and talk about him. First, have you got a photograph of him?"

"No."

"Not even a snapshot?"

"No."

"Then will you describe him to me?"

They went back to the sitting-room and sat down in the chairs in which they had sat before and he took a notebook from a pocket. Rachel could see Ian in her mind as clearly as if he had been standing in the room with them, but when she tried to describe him it seemed extraordinarily difficult.

"He isn't very tall," she said. "Just two or three inches taller than me. And he's quite slim. And he's got dark hair, almost black and quite straight. His eyes are dark and his features—well, his nose is what I think you'd call aquiline and he's got a sharpish chin and very good teeth. I don't know what he might have been wearing, because I don't know what he'd have worn in this climate."

The sergeant had been writing while she talked and for a moment he said nothing as if he were waiting for her to add something to her description. When she did not he eyed her in a dubious manner, handling his chin again, which she had noticed was one of his mannerisms.

"This is your brother you're describing?" he said.

"Yes, of course," she answered.

"You can't add anything else, some distinctive mark, a scar or a mole or anything?"

"No, I don't think so."

"The odd thing is," he said, "that it's a perfect description of Constoupolis."

CHAPTER 8

She thought about it and had to admit that it was.

"But they aren't in the least alike," she said. "You could never mistake one for the other."

"That may be so," he said. "Descriptions of people can be extraordinarily misleading. That's why I asked you if there wasn't something really distinctive about your brother. Not only on his face, but on his body, because it may be—" He stopped himself abruptly, but his doubtful gaze remained on her face.

She finished his sentence for him in a bitter voice. "It may be it's his body you're going to find, if you ever find him. But I can't think of anything special and I never saw Mr. Constoupolis unclothed, so I can't tell you if he had any distinguishing marks or not."

His mouth tilted up once more at the corner. "A bit fond of sarcasm, aren't you, Miss Gairdner?" he said. "I only want to help you, you know."

"But why is it important that their descriptions should sound rather alike?" she asked. "I expect they'd fit lots of people."

"I don't know," he answered. "Perhaps it isn't important. It's only something that struck me as strange while you were talking."

"But as I told you, they're completely unlike."

"Right. Then let's go on to the next thing. What's your brother's occupation?"

"He works for a firm called Ledyard Groome and Company who make agricultural machinery. It's a British-owned company, but they have several branches in Australia. The managing director here is a man called Andrew Wellman."

She could see no sign that the name meant anything to him, but he wrote it down in his notebook.

"Do you know him?" he asked.

"No, but as a matter of fact . . ." She hesitated, then decided to go on. "I met his son yesterday. His name is Peter. He came round here in the afternoon to see Ian, who I gather is a friend of his, and he stayed chatting for a time. He didn't know anything about what had happened to Ian and I think he was worried about him."

"He works for the firm, I suppose."

"No, he doesn't. And I don't think he lives with his parents either. He says he's a writer."

"Is he the only person, apart from the Greeks, you've seen since you got here?"

"Actually, no. Earlier in the afternoon there was a man . . ." She tried to keep her recollections in order and to make sure that she did not blunder into talking about the drugged wine or Dr. Rayne. "Does the name Slattery mean anything to you?"

For an instant, because of a startled gleam that she was certain she saw in his eyes, she was sure that it did, but at once his gaze became as unrevealing as before, interested, attentive, yet a little doubtful and giving nothing away of what he thought of her situation.

"I don't think so," he said. "Why?"

"It's only that a man who said his name was Slattery came here in the afternoon and said he'd an appointment with Alex Constoupolis. And when I said he and Maria had gone way to Mildura for the week-end he didn't believe me and he forced his way into the house and went right through it, looking for them. To tell the truth, I was rather frightened of him, but once he was sure that Alex and Maria had really gone away he just went away himself."

"Can you describe him?"

Oddly enough, she found it easier to describe a man whom she had seen only once and that very briefly than someone like Ian whom she knew intimately. She described the man's height and breadth, his large face with the cluster of small features in the middle of it, his crisply curling light brown hair and bushy eyebrows and his paunch that hung out over the belt that held up his trousers. The sergeant made notes while she talked.

"I'll check and see if we've anything on him," he said. "It doesn't ring a bell at the moment."

But she was sure that it had rung a bell and wished that she could see what he had written in his notebook. At this point, however, he closed it and returned it to a pocket. He stood up.

"We'll be in touch," he said. "I hope we can help. If you hear anything yourself, of course, you'll let us know."

"Of course."

"How were things last night? No trouble here?"

For a moment she felt that he must know all about the wine and about the visit of David Rayne and his mother and that that could only mean that after all the doctor had not treated the events of the night as a professional confidence, but had already told the police about them.

Then she had second thoughts, beginning to wonder if she had misunderstood the sergeant's question.

"Trouble?" she said. "What do you mean?"

"Only that there was a bit of a riot along by the jetty," he said. "Nothing much. A few kids throwing stones and making a nuisance of themselves. High on drugs, mostly. A few people got hurt but we didn't make any arrests. But I know there'll be people who say the police overreacted and were really the cause of the trouble, and there'll be other people who say we didn't crack down nearly hard enough on the trouble-makers. It's what always happens."

"High on drugs?" Rachel said. "Addicts, do you mean?"

He nodded. "Yes, it's a major problem among adolescents here, just as it is in most other parts of the world. But you didn't hear any of the racket along here?"

"No, I was asleep." And how deeply asleep she had been, also drugged. "Where do the drugs come from?"

"Indonesia, mostly. And there are all kinds of places where it can get into the country. We've an immense coastline. It can't be patrolled all the time. From time to time we pull in one of the distributors, but the traffic goes on. Funny thing, I can't remember ever wanting anything of the kind myself when I was a kid. Just a few cheap cigarettes in secret with one's mates behind some bushes. And now they're saying that's almost as dangerous as cannabis. I gave up smoking myself because I couldn't afford it. Goodbye now, Miss Gairdner. I hope we get some good news for you soon and I hope you have a happy visit in Australia."

Rachel saw him to the front door and closed it behind him.

Soon after he had gone she opened it again and let the dogs into the house and fed them and thought that presently she would take them for a walk. She thought too about what Sergeant Ross had told her of the riot at the jetty the evening before and wondered if he had had any motive in talking about it. Did he want her to think about drugs? Was he hinting that there could be some connection between drugs and Ian's disappearance, or at least the sudden departure of the Constoupolises and the visit of Slattery?

The sergeant did not know Ian, so he could not know how fantastic it would be to connect him with drug smuggling, but with the Greeks and Slattery it might be another matter. And might it not be possible, if they were connected with the evil traffic, that Ian, being in this house, had stumbled across something that was dangerous to them and had been dealt with?

Fear came surging back. Then, after fear for Ian, came fear for herself. Someone, it seemed certain, had tried to murder her last night, but had bungled it because whoever did it had not known enough about a drug called Somnolin. But even if Ian had somehow disastrously become a danger to a ring of drug smugglers, why should anyone think that she could be a danger to them? And who could have written that letter? Who knew about Hamish? Who knew that Ian and Eudora were likely to get married?

The answers to those last two questions were all too simple. Ian and Eudora.

And Eudora knew that Rachel had inherited a fair amount of money recently and that Ian was sure to be her heir. And it had to be faced, Ian knew it too. A sudden nightmare engulfed Rachel's consciousness, wide awake as she was. It was the thought that, whatever her private feelings about him were, it could have been Ian who had come to the bungalow either while she had been asleep or out with the dogs, poisoned the wine, then returned in the night to place the forged suicide note beside her. And his disappearance could be merely part of constructing an alibi for the time of her death.

She picked up the letter from where it lay on her dressing-table and read it again.

Seeing it in daylight and with her brain no longer fogged by the drug that she had taken, she saw that it was not at all a clever forgery. It was a very crude one. The writing bore only a superficial resemblance to her own. Anyone, let alone an expert, who compared it with a letter really written by her, could easily recognize the difference.

When she next saw David Rayne, she thought, she would show him a letter which she acknowledged was one of hers and let him compare it with the one that he had found. Somewhere in Ian's room, she was sure, she would find some of the letters that she had sent him, for he was one of the people who almost never throw letters away, and if she let the doctor put the two letters side by side, he would be positively convinced at last, as she was half afraid that he might not be even now, that she had neither tried to kill herself nor faked a suicide.

In the mood that she was in, she felt very like picking up the telephone once more and asking the doctor to come back to the bungalow so that she could prove her point. But she controlled the impulse, thinking that if she did it at all it should be later in the day. At the moment, she thought, he had probably the feeling that having sat up with her for most of the night, he had had enough of her to be going on with. The best thing to do would be to take the dogs for a walk.

But she idled the morning away, presently having some bread and cheese for her lunch and only then, after making sure that this time she had the key of the front door in her handbag and that the back door was locked, fastening the dogs' leads to their collars and setting out.

The sun was very hot and had a great, almost bronze-coloured circle around it in the sky. She stood staring at it for a moment. She had never seen anything like it before. It seemed to her that there was something ominous about it, almost sinister. When she reached the beach she was taken utterly by surprise. The day before there had been a crowd around the jetty, but today the crowds were everywhere. The strip of grass between the road and the sandy shore was completely covered by row on row of small, brightly coloured tents in which girls in bikinis and young men in even scantier clothing were sheltering from the heat of the sun. In a number of the tents there were radios pouring out music, fortunately not as loud as that of the day before, but making a fair cacophony, and small children, some of them quite naked, wandering about from tent to tent, apparently studying with interest the ways in which their elders took their leisure.

There were also a good many tents and umbrellas set up on the beach, with family groups sitting here and there and children of various ages playing the inevitable cricket wherever they could find room for it. A lot of people were in the water, swimming or simply splashing about. They all seemed to be enjoying themselves, yet an absurd feeling came to Rachel that the scene before her was somehow like pictures that she had seen of refugee camps in some of the more desolate parts of the world. It was because of those tents, packed so tightly together and so densely filled with people. These people, of course, looked healthy and well nourished, some, indeed, to go by the plumpness of their tanned bodies, positively overfed, but it was a happy, colourful picture.

Unfortunately for Rachel, however, she always shrank from packed crowds of people, even when they looked peaceful and contented. An almost claustrophobic panic gripped her now and she hurried the dogs along, passing the bench where she had sat the day before with Mrs. Rayne and on along the road till she reached the jetty.

She turned to the right there, then after a short distance to the right again, and soon found herself back in Bessborough Street and saw that a car was parked in front of No. 21.

It was the same cream-coloured Peugeot in which Pete Wellman had arrived the day before. The garden gate was open and two people were at the front door, looking as if they were waiting for it to be opened after they had rung the bell. One was Pete. The other was a tall woman, slim, erect, grey-haired and about fifty years old. As soon as the dogs saw them they set up their usual noise barking and started tugging at their leads, and though Rachel told them to be quiet, they did not take much notice of her. If they had accepted her on friendly terms, they did not recognize her authority over them.

Pete came towards her along the garden path.

"Hallo," he said. "This is my mother, Sara. I've told her about Ian going missing and she wants to know if she can help in any way. I suppose you still haven't heard from him."

"No," Rachel said, "there's been nothing."

"It's an extraordinary thing," the tall woman said. "I don't know him very well, but from what I do it seems so unlike him."

She was wearing a short sleeveless cotton dress of bright scarlet, white sandals and a chain of big white beads round her throat. Her face and her bare arms and legs were deeply tanned. Her face had neat, sharply defined features and big, grey, gentle-looking eyes that were the only things about her that resembled her son, though there was a trace of melancholy in hers that was not there in his. Her grey hair was wispy and in spite of her fine bones there was a curiously abrupt gaucherie about her. Her smile was diffident, as if she were naturally a shy person who found it difficult to make advances to a stranger.

"The police have been in touch with me and told me about it," she said, sounding as if she were making an apology for this. "A man called Ross came to see me. He wanted my husband, but he's at our house on Hindmarsh Island. I was just leaving to go there myself when the man came and when I heard what it was all about I thought I ought to stay in case I could help. Actually Pete told me about it before the police came, but I didn't realize how serious it was until they did. I'm so very sorry about it. It's a dreadful way to welcome you to this country."

"It's very kind of you to come," Rachel said. "Come in, won't you?"

She unlocked the door and the three of them went into the house.

As she went in Rachel realized that she was listening for a sound of some sort, as if she half expected Ian to have returned during her short absence. Yet at the same time it struck her that there was something unreal about this expectation, that her deeper feeling was almost the opposite, that it would have astonished her intensely if he had been there. During the day a sense had been growing in her that there was no point in going on expecting him, because very likely he would never reappear. This was not quite conscious, yet it created a darkness at the back of her mind.

"Would you like some tea?" she asked. "I'm quite good now at finding my way about the kitchen."

"Oh, no, please don't bother," Sara Wellman said. She had sat down. "Is it true that the Greek couple have gone away and that you're here by yourself?"

"Yes, for the moment," Rachel replied.

"I thought so, and I hate the thought of you being here all alone, and I thought perhaps you'd like to come to the island with us. Won't you do that? It isn't very far and we could always get you back quite quickly if for some reason you're needed."

There was a good deal of attraction for Rachel in the suggestion. She had begun to feel a sort of hatred of this bungalow.

But she said, "It's wonderfully kind of you. There's nothing I'd like better. Only I think I ought to stay in case Ian suddenly comes back, or in case there's a telephone call from the police about him, or anything like that."

"You could leave a note for him here to say where you were," Sara Wellman said. "He knows the house on the island and he could come out there himself. We've plenty of room. And we could telephone the police to tell them where you are."

"But suppose he's ill," Rachel said, "or perhaps— Well, one of the things I've wondered about is whether he might have had a loss of memory, for instance, if he's been in an accident, and then, if he got home, he might not be able to cope. It's really good of you and I'm immensely grateful, but I think I ought to stay here."

"Incidentally, how are you yourself?" Pete asked. "Did you have a good night?"

He had not sat down but was standing in front of the window with his hands in his pockets. As Rachel turned her head towards him and his eyes met hers he seemed to be sending her some sort of signal, but she was not sure what it was."

"Yes, thank you," she said. "Did you?"

"Couldn't have been worse," he answered. "I was sick over and over again. It must have been something I had to eat or drink yesterday. I wondered about you, in case it was that wine we had together. I thought it might have been tainted in some way. But if you'd no trouble from it, it must have been something else I had."

He was telling her, however, that he knew it had been the wine, but also that he had not told his mother about it.

Rachel did not need telling how much he knew, for David Rayne must have given him some explanation of why he had happened to ring him up at four in the morning. But why Pete had chosen not to tell his mother what had happened Rachel did not know. Of course it might have been that he was leaving it to her to say something about it or not, as she chose. That probably explained the look in his eyes that had struck her as a signal.

"You eat too much of that take-away food," Sara Wellman said. "It's often a bit off. And it's fattening too. If only you'd be sensible and live at home you could have wholesome food and not put on weight. I'm sure you've put on some weight since I saw you last."

He strolled towards her, put a hand on her shoulder, stooped and kissed her on the cheek.

"Darling, we've been into all that over and over again,

haven't we?" he said. "You know I and the old man drive each other mad."

"He's very fond of you, you know he is," she said.

"D'you mean it?" he said sceptically. "Then why can't he let me go my own way?"

"Because he thinks at your age you ought to be in a job, you ought to work. And I'm sure he's right."

He patted her shoulder again. "You aren't really. You know I'm doing the best thing. And I work very hard. Writing is as hard work as any you can find."

"If only you could get something published . . ." She sighed. She turned back to Rachel with one of her diffident smiles. "I'm sorry, we shouldn't be arguing about this sort of thing in front of you, but it's an old family quarrel. Pete and my husband have never agreed about these things. Andy could get Pete a job in the firm, like Ian's, and he could earn a good salary and live with us and be properly looked after, at least until he marries, instead of living in a bed-sitting-room and eating all that fish and chips and that Chinese food and those curries and things, and having terrible upsets, like last night. But he'd sooner live on the dole. Just think of it—the dole!"

"And a bit of grape-picking if I'm short of cash," Pete said. "I enjoy that. And I don't ever bother you for money, do I?"

"No," she admitted. "Sometimes I almost wish you would. You wouldn't feel so lost to us."

"Darling, if it was only you at home, you know I'd move in with you tomorrow and exploit your generosity to the limit," he said. "But Andy and I just don't talk the same language. When I stay with you I soon start feeling the house is full of hate. I'm not exaggerating. Really I do and I can't bear it. Andy would sooner I didn't exist. He can't understand that a writer's got a job to learn, the same as everyone else, and while he's doing it he needs peace and quiet to do it in. It would be no use to me to go to an office every day and turn into a sort of salesman."

"I'm sure all sorts of writers have had jobs of different kinds before they really got ahead with their writing," his mother said, "and I expect they benefitted by their experiences."

"I imagine some did, some didn't," he said. "I'm one of the ones who wouldn't. What I really wish is that I had a nice safe private income, left me by some beneficent aunt, then you wouldn't feel ashamed of me, as you do about that dole, though it would come to much the same thing, wouldn't it?" He looked at Rachel. "Don't you agree with me?"

So Ian must have talked to him about her legacy from Aunt Christina, she thought, and it rather dismayed her that he had.

"Perhaps," she said noncommittally.

She was thinking that there was obviously a great deal of affection between this mother and son, even if the father and son were unable to agree.

"Anyway, I'm coming out to Hindmarsh Island with you today, aren't I?" he said to his mother. "I only hope I don't ruin the holiday for you."

"Of course you won't," she said. "You've only got to be a little tactful. Don't behave as if you despise Andy for having worked so hard all his life. D'you know, Pete, I sometimes feel there's almost a sort of snobbery about your attitude, as if you were a little aristocrat who doesn't need to earn money, while Andy's just a poor working man."

"Darling, don't talk nonsense," he said. "I respect him enormously, even if he hates me."

She turned back to Rachel. "Do think again about coming out to the island with us, Miss Gairdner. We should so love to have you and I'm really not happy about you staying on here all by yourself."

"I'm truly grateful for the invitation, Mrs. Wellman,"

Rachel replied. "But among the other problems, you see, is the fact that I've got to look after the Constoupolises' dogs. I can't let them down about that."

The front-door bell rang.

It seemed to startle them all. Sara and Pete Wellman looked as surprised that Rachel should be having a visitor as she felt herself. She did not think that this time it could be Ian. She had had the delusion once before when she heard the bell and was not led astray by it again. But she could not think of who else it could be unless it was David Rayne. Unless, of course, it was that man Slattery once more.

She felt a mixture of disappointment, relief and alarm when, on opening the door, she saw that it was Sergeant Ross on the doorstep. The alarm was because she could think of no reason why he should have come unless it was to bring bad news.

"So you've heard something about my brother," she said. "Is that it?"

"No, not exactly," he answered. "But we've found out something of interest. Perhaps if I could come in . . ."

"Oh yes, I'm sorry, do come in." She stood aside for him to enter and took him into the sitting-room. "I believe you've met Mrs. Wellman."

"That's right," he said. "Good afternoon, Mrs. Wellman." Then he spoke again to Rachel. "We've discovered a strange thing, Miss Gairdner. Your friends the Greeks didn't set off for Mildura at all. They left for home. They had to change at Perth and Singapore on the flight they took, but by now they'll be in Athens."

CHAPTER 9

Rachel did not know why he should describe the Constou-polises as her friends, except that when people speak of "your friends" in a certain tone of voice they usually mean it to be derogatory.

"What does that mean?" she asked.

"At a guess," he said, "it means they got frightened and bolted for their lives."

"Frightened of what?"

"Frightened when you arrived here without your brother and they realized that he'd really disappeared. Until that happened, they may have been hanging on, hoping for the best."

"You still aren't saying what they were frightened of."

"Well, no, I suppose I'm not. It isn't too easy to explain. The fact is, we know a bit more about that couple than I've told you. Drugs, you know. Heroin. That was their line. They were distributors locally. We got onto them a little while ago and to save themselves they were going to talk, and if anyone in the gang they were working with found that out their lives wouldn't be worth much. So they packed up and ran for it—taking their winter clothes, of course, and leaving their summer things behind."

"I don't understand," Rachel said. "What could that possibly have had to do with my brother? If you're going to say he was involved in drug smuggling I shan't believe a word of it."

"No doubt he wasn't," the sergeant replied. "But do you

remember, when you described your brother to me, I said you could have been describing Constoupolis?"

"And I told you there wasn't the slightest resemblance between them."

"Oh yes, it's possible there wasn't. But imagine you've been sent here to pick up Constoupolis, whom you've never seen. You've only been given a description of him. And you're keeping an eye on the house and you see a short, thin, dark man with aquiline features come out of it, wouldn't you be sure that that was your man? And you'd follow him and when the opportunity came you'd bundle him into your car, probably knock him unconscious and take off with him. Sooner or later, of course, you'd discover your mistake. Someone who knew Constoupolis would tell you you'd got the wrong man."

"And then?"

Rachel heard her voice rise sharply with the note of hysteria in it that frightened her.

"Then the Constoupolises realized what had happened, packed all they could in a hurry, leaving the mess behind them that you saw, and took off for Athens."

"I mean," Rachel said, speaking with careful control, "what happened to Ian?"

He made a little gesture of helplessness. She thought that it really distressed him to have to say what he must.

"I wish I could tell you something to cheer you, but if he was abducted by drug smugglers and by now knows enough about them to be dangerous to them, I'm very afraid you've got to face the possibility that he hasn't—well, survived."

"That he's dead," she said harshly.

"Yes, that's what I mean," he admitted reluctantly. "It could be."

"Listen!" Pete suddenly broke in excitedly. His big grey eyes seemed to have become even larger in his softly un-finished face. "If you're right, if I've understood half of

what you're talking about, then someone gave these kidnappers a description of Alex Constoupolis, but it must
have been to someone who didn't know Ian. Who could
that be?"

"Slattery!" Rachel exclaimed.

The three other people in the room all turned to look at
her.

She began a hurried explanation. "He was someone who
came here yesterday, looking for Alex. He forced his way
into the house and wouldn't go away till he'd made sure
the Constoupolises weren't here. I can see him abducting
—oh no, that won't do. He knew Alex and he'd met Ian, at
least he said he had, so he'd never have made that mistake."

"But mightn't he be the person who described Alex to
his bosses, whoever they are?" Pete said. "The sergeant
said that when you described Ian to him you could have
been describing Alex, though, as you said, there's no resemblance between them. I know myself there isn't. But
this man—what did you say his name was?"

"Slattery," Rachel said.

"Couldn't this man Slattery have described Alex without realizing that he was describing Ian too?"

Ross nodded. "Just what I was going to say myself. We're
on the look-out for him and we'll pick him up sooner or
later, but meanwhile—well, Miss Gairdner, I wish I had
better news for you, but I shouldn't give up hope en-
tirely."

"Rachel—" Sara Wellman began. She stood up and put
an arm round Rachel's shoulders. "After this you aren't
staying here by yourself. You're coming out to Hindmarsh
Island with us. There's nothing against her going there
with us, is there, Sergeant?"

"Nothing at all," he replied, "if you leave us your address and telephone number, in case we have any news for
her."

"It's very good of you to suggest it," Rachel said, "but all the same . . ." She paused because she did not know what she wanted to say. After a moment she went on, "I can't leave the dogs, you see."

"That's no problem, we'll take them with us," Sara said. "It'll be fine for them. They can run loose, there's no traffic. So just go and pack a few things and come along. I couldn't rest, thinking of you here alone after what's happened. If you really don't want to come, I'll move in with you for the next few days. I've got my case in the car, so it shouldn't be difficult. But really I think you'd like it on the island and that coming along with Pete and me would be the best thing you could do."

"Thank you very much, then," Rachel said. "I'll come, if you really don't mind the dogs."

"I love dogs," Sara said.

"But what will become of them, I wonder, if the Constoupolises have gone to Athens and aren't coming back?" Rachel said. "I can't very well adopt them for life. Sooner or later I shall have to go home to Scotland."

"I'm sure we can find a good home for them when the time comes," Sara said. "Sergeant, you said you want my address and telephone number on Hindmarsh Island."

"Please." He took his notebook from his pocket and jotted down the address and number that she gave him.

"Is that all, then?" she asked. "Can we go now?"

"Why not?" he said.

"Then go and pack," she said to Rachel, "and we'll be going."

"Sergeant—" Rachel began.

"Yes?" he said.

"Please, don't you know anything, anything at all, about who might have abducted Ian?"

She thought that she saw a look on his face as if he were about to tell her something more than he had told her so far, but then he shook his head.

"Not really, Miss Gairdner," he said. "I might make a dozen guesses and not one of them be right. Just trust us to do the best we can and to let you know immediately the moment we know anything. But as I said—"

"I know, I know!" She hurried out of the room before he could repeat that he had very little hope that they would find Ian alive.

The drive to Hindmarsh Island took about an hour and a half. Pete drove and Rachel sat beside him. Sara sat on the back seat with the two dogs. They appeared to like being driven as long as they both had the opportunity of looking out of a window of the car, seeming to take a lively interest in the scenery through which they were passing.

They were heading, Pete explained, to the town of Goolwa, where they would drive onto a ferry that would take them to the island. On the way to Goolwa they passed between low hills, formed in smooth folds and with the grass on them burnt to a sandy brown by the heat of the summer. For most of the time the road was a long, empty stretch with almost no traffic on it. The sun was beginning to sink and there were flecks of pink in the sky, which was not as deeply blue as it had been earlier in the day but was beginning to show the first faint pallor of evening.

Goolwa was a small, quiet township through which the road led to the ferry. There were already four or five cars on it and the ferryman was just about to close it off, preparatory to leaving for the island, when Pete drove up. He was allowed to drive onto the wide, solid-looking boat, he and the ferryman exchanging greetings as he did so, then the barrier across the road behind them was dropped, a loud, clanking noise began and the ferry edged its way out into the river.

"D'you know, there isn't a single policeman on Hindmarsh Island," Sara said. "That man there has the power of arrest if trouble breaks out on the ferry, but I don't believe he's ever had to use it. We're a very law-abiding lot here."

The clanking went on for only a few minutes, then stopped.

"Well, here we are," Pete said and, as a barrier ahead of them was lifted, drove off the ferry once more onto dry land.

The Wellmans' house was a roomy, single-storey building which faced across a mass of reeds and beyond them the river. There was a pale reflection in the water of the pink that was spreading in the sky. There was only one other house near, a bungalow about a hundred yards farther on along the quiet road. A wide pathway, mostly covered in grass, ran between the densely growing reeds to the water's edge, and near the end of the path a boat was moored.

Two people were in it, looking as if they might have been busy with some cleaning-up operation, but at the moment they were standing facing one another, intent on each other, as if in the middle of a fierce argument or some other emotional exchange. When they heard the car stop in the road they both turned, waved, then climbed out of the boat on to the pathway and came up to the road.

Sara let the dogs out of the car before climbing out herself. They both went wild, dashing off along the road, barking with excitement. Rachel and Pete stepped out of the car beside Sara.

She said to Rachel, "Andy, my husband. And Eudora Linley. She's Andy's secretary and a great friend of ours. I'm so glad you've had the chance to meet. Andy, this is Rachel."

"Glad to meet you, Rachel," Andrew Wellman said. "But where's Ian?"

He was a big man of about fifty, tall and wide-shouldered, with grey hair trimmed very short and a tanned, leathery-looking face. For a moment, as he and Rachel

shook hands, she had an impression that there was a re-
markable resemblance between him and Pete, but almost
at once her sense of this faded. There might be a likeness
between their features, though those of the older man,
while having something of the blurred, unformed quality
of his son's, were both coarser and stronger, but their eyes
were totally dissimilar.

Pete had inherited his gentle, innocent eyes from his
mother. His father's were also grey, but they were small
and deep-set and looked sharply observant. They looked
wary, almost suspicious. Certainly he did not look as if he
would ever be inclined to take anyone on trust. Rachel felt
him scrutinizing her with a gaze that did not commit him
to showing either approval or disapproval. He was wearing shorts which showed his long, muscular, hairy legs and
a faded blue shirt with its sleeves rolled up.

"Hasn't Eudora told you all about that?" Sara said. "It's
very distressing. Let's go inside."

Rachel was looking past Andrew Wellman at Eudora, far
more interested in her than in her host. The girl was about
twenty-five, tall and slim, with a curious air of radiance
about her, a kind of brilliance, and far from seeming to
want to use this to make an impression, she appeared
almost to be trying to conceal it. She had a look about her
of a kind of nervous excitability that might lead her, at any
slight provocation, to burst into delightful laughter or just
as probably break into tears. She moved with a light, free
vitality and had a smooth oval face, light brown hair to her
shoulders and dark blue eyes. She also was wearing shorts,
but the legs they revealed were slender and very elegant,
and she was wearing no shirt but only a narrow, bright
orange brassiere.

She adopted the dogs at once with enthusiasm and she
seemed to be the member of the party that they favoured.
With Pete taking all the luggage that had been brought
out of the car, they all went indoors, entering a big sitting-

room, one end of which had been converted into a kitchen, with a refrigerator and an electric cooking-stove and a number of cupboards. The room was very simply but comfortably furnished, with several framed photographs which Rachel supposed were of scenes on the island, hanging on the pale grey walls. There was a vase of some attractive sweet-scented flowers of which Rachel did not know the name on the table.

"You mean you still haven't heard anything of Ian?" Andrew Wellman said, looking curiously at Rachel. "Haven't you any idea yet what's happened to him?"

Sara answered for her. "None at all. But I'm going to show Rachel her room, then we can talk."

She took Rachel through a door that opened out of the sitting-room onto a passage and to a room at the end of it. Pete followed them with Rachel's suitcase. The room was small and bright, with a bed that had a counterpane with a design on it which Rachel thought must be aboriginal, and a built-in cupboard and dressing-table. Sara showed her where the bathroom was and told her to join the rest of them in the sitting-room when she was ready.

Rachel went after Sara almost at once and heard her say to Andrew, "There's been a disturbing development which I don't think Eudora could have told you about. The Constoupolises—you know, the Greek couple with whom Ian was lodging—they've disappeared, after saying that they were flying up to Mildura for the holiday, and the police have found out that they didn't go to Mildura at all, but took off for Athens. And the police, that's to say, a very polite sergeant called Ross, say they were involved in distributing drugs and were going to talk about where they were coming from, and that their bosses found out about this, and Ian may have been abducted in mistake for Alex Constoupolis, and so—and so—" She stopped and suddenly put an arm round Rachel. "When these people find they've made a mistake they'll turn him loose and the police will find him and everything will be all right."

"Christ!" Andrew Wellman exploded. "You mean they really think he's probably been murdered?"

"Andy!" Sara cried, her voice full of reproach. "To say a thing like that to the poor girl!"

"It's all right," Rachel said. "I'd sooner we said it. It's better to face it than to pretend it couldn't have happened."

"That's the spirit," Andrew said. "But what a hell of a welcome to give you to this country. It isn't always like this, you know. We usually do our best to give our visitors a good time."

"Oh yes, we can be quite civilized," Eudora said. She sounded as if she thought that she had made a joke and felt inclined to titter. "But Ian's such a simpleton. If a strange man came up to him and said, "Get in my car," without telling him why, it's just what Ian would do. He'd think it was an old Australian custom and that he might offend the natives if he refused."

"Well, I'm glad Sara brought you out here," Andrew said. "I shouldn't like to think of you sleeping alone in that house." He turned back to his wife. "What have we got to eat? Have you brought anything with you?"

"I've brought a cold chicken and some salad and some cheese and some watermelon," she answered.

"And we've plenty of drinks here. You see," he went on to Rachel, "we haven't any shops on the island. When we stay here we bring most of our supplies with us. Now then, if you feel like it, I could take you a short trip around the island while Sara's getting the tea. Would you like that? Don't hesitate to say no if you'd rather not."

Rachel saw that he was anxious to do something which he thought might help to distract her, so she felt that she ought to be grateful and said that she would very much enjoy a trip round the island.

"Good," he said. "Then come along." He looked at Eudora. "Coming too?"

"Thank you, no," she said with a little smile, as if it gave her some kind of pleasure to reject his offer. "I'll stay and help Sara."

He did not invite Pete to accompany them. This did not strike Rachel at the moment, but as she and Andrew went out to the car she found herself wondering about the nature of the relationship between the father and son. Since Pete's arrival at the house he and Andrew had not exchanged a word and had hardly even glanced at one another. If Pete was devoted to his mother, as Rachel believed he was, it looked as if he and his father could very well do without one another.

The trip around the island on which Andrew took her began by his driving straight on past the neighbouring bungalow and staying on the road that ran parallel to the river. Thick beds of reeds edged the water and Andrew told her that until he had himself had the path made that ran through them to where the boat was moored, he and Sara had had to force their way through them, sometimes sinking knee-deep into the marsh out of which they grew, sometimes encountering snakes.

The island was almost flat and at some time of the year would have been green, but at present, like the hills that Rachel had seen on the way to Goolwa, the fields were burnt a tawny brown by the heat of the summer. There were pine trees down the middle of the island and cattle in the fields. Andrew called them simply beef, as if they had no existence prior to their arrival at the butcher's. The sunset was spreading now, making great splashes of fiery opalescence across the sky and what was left of the blue in it was a deep, wonderful shade of turquoise.

At the bottom of a rough flight of steps that led up to the top of a low ridge, Andrew stopped the car and said, "You might like to take a look from up there. It's quite a sight."

They both got out of the car. It surprised Rachel how strongly the wind was blowing. She had been unaware of any when they were still at the house, but here it tore at her hair and her skirt with unexpected strength and a pleasant coolness.

She and Andrew climbed the steps. From the top she saw the island stretching out beyond them for some way, but at what seemed to be the end of it immense breakers came riding in from the sea, which was visible from this point, and crashing down with a high white boiling of surf. There was fascination in standing there letting the rhythm of the great breakers almost hypnotize her.

Standing beside her, Andrew said, "That's where the river meets the sea."

"Could a boat get in from the sea?" she asked out of curiosity. "I suppose not."

"Well, it's been done, I happen to know," he answered, "but it's very dangerous. Why d'you ask?"

"I just wondered."

"It needs a catamaran," he said. "The river here's very shallow, so it's got to be something with a very shallow draught. You come along there"—he pointed—"that's the Coorong, till you get to the Tawitchere Barrage, and you go through that to the entrance of Lake Alexandrina. That's a big lake to the north of the island. Then you go past the Clayton Cliffs over there"—he pointed again—"and into the Murray proper. And after that it's easy till you get to the Goolwa ferry. Of course, if you want to slip in unnoticed . . ." He paused.

"Yes?" Rachel said.

"The thing would be to stick to the south of the island. You'd have to go through a lock to get to Goolwa, but it's unmanned. You handle it yourself. So you could get through it and land on the island without anyone knowing where you'd come from. Risky, of course, but possible."

She looked at him curiously. He was not looking at her,

but out towards the thundering surf. She thought how strange it was that there should be so much resemblance and yet so much difference between him and his son. As long as she could not see his small, suspicious eyes the resemblance seemed strong, but when he turned and looked at her again it vanished.

"Better be getting home now," he said. "Feel like a drink? There'll be time for one before tea."

They went down the steps and got back into the car and started back towards the Wellmans' house.

Just before they reached it something happened which made Rachel wonder for a moment if she might be going out of her mind. They were passing the bungalow which was nearest to the Wellmans', a very similar building, modern and pleasantly designed and set in a small, neat garden, and at its open door stood a man.

The man was Slattery.

She saw him clearly. It was Slattery unquestionably. But in a moment he was gone.

"That man—!" she exclaimed excitedly. "Did you see him?"

"Who?" Andrew asked.

"That man in the doorway. Oh, do stop!"

"I didn't see anyone," Andrew said.

He did not stop.

"It was Slattery, I'm sure it was."

"Who's Slattery?"

It took her a moment to remember that the Wellmans knew very little about what had happened at Bessborough Street since her arrival. She did not think that she had spoken of Slattery even to Pete.

"Who lives in that house?" she asked. "It isn't a man called Slattery?"

"Never heard of him," he answered. "Our neighbours are a young couple called Pringle who moved into the house a few months ago. We don't know much about them.

They aren't very friendly. I don't mean we've ever had any trouble with them, they just like to keep themselves to themselves. And so do we when we're out here, so that suits us all right."

"The man isn't a big fat man with funny little features in the middle of a big fat face?"

"No, he's tall and rather thin and Eudora, who notices such things, says he's very good-looking. I can't give much of an opinion on that myself."

She sighed. "Perhaps I didn't see him. Perhaps it's just that he's so much on my mind that I'm liable to see him everywhere."

The car had stopped in front of the Wellmans' house. Andrew got out and opened the door for her.

"Want to tell us just why he's so much on your mind, whoever he is?" he asked.

She thought that there was even more suspicion than usual in the hard gaze that he let dwell on her face.

"Perhaps I should," she said.

"Come along in, then, and let's have that drink."

They went together into the sitting-room.

CHAPTER 10

The dogs gave Rachel a welcome as if she were their oldest and best friend who had been away for a month. It took some moments to persuade them to settle down again.

A meal had already been laid out on the table: a chicken, a bowl of salad and bread and butter. There were cheese and some slices of water-melon on a sideboard. Eudora and Pete already had drinks in their hands. Eudora had put on a white shirt over her orange brassiere and had tied her hair back with a ribbon, and as she lounged in a chair with her long, elegant legs crossed it struck Rachel even more strongly than before how extraordinarily attractive she was. If Ian had been in constant contact with her in the office where they both worked, she thought, it was inevitable that he should have fallen in love with her.

"Rachel's going to tell us something peculiar about our neighbours," Andrew said. "But a drink for her first. What's it to be, Rachel? Whisky, sherry, some white wine?"

She chose the white wine and he poured out a glass for her and some whisky with water and ice for himself. Sara had some orange juice, saying with one of her diffident smiles and sounding almost apologetic about it that she hardly ever touched alcohol.

"Now go ahead, Rachel," Andrew said when they had all sat down. "What is it you think you saw?"

"I did see him." She had been considering the matter. "I'm sure I did."

"Right. Then tell us who he is and why you're worried about him."

"It's complicated," she said. "I don't know quite where to begin. You see, when I arrived in Adelaide yesterday and Ian wasn't there to meet me, and when I got to the house where he's been staying and he wasn't there either, I began to get very worried, but all the same I had a shower and went to bed and went to sleep. Then I woke up in the middle of the afternoon—your afternoon, I mean, of course—I don't know what time of day I felt it was. And I found that except for me and the dogs the house was empty. Well, actually the dogs were in the garden, but Ian hadn't come home and the Constoupolises, who own the house, weren't there either. They'd just left a note for me, with a bottle of wine, on the kitchen table, and the note said they'd left for Mildura that afternoon instead of waiting till next day and that there was food in the fridge and so on. And then the doorbell rang and there was a man there who said he'd an appointment with Alex Constoupolis and he said his name was Slattery. And when I said Alex and Maria had gone away he forced his way into the house and insisted on going through it to make sure they really weren't there. And that's the man I had just a glimpse of a few minutes ago in your neighbours' doorway."

"Now wait a minute," Andrew said. "Out there you said perhaps you only thought you'd seen him, you weren't sure about it."

"I know I did," Rachel said. "It seemed so strange. But really I'm quite sure I saw him."

Pete was watching her with his gentle but perceptive gaze. "You haven't told us the whole story yet, have you, Rachel?"

"Well, no," she admitted.

"Why don't you?" he said. "It might do you good. I should, if I were you."

She was not at all sure that she wanted to go on, but the way that Pete was watching her put a kind of pressure on her and suddenly she decided to take the plunge. The load of discretion was becoming too much for her.

"Some other queer things happened yesterday," she said. "Pete could tell you about some of them. He came to see me and we had a drink together out of the bottle of wine the Constoupolises had left on the kitchen table. Soon after he left I fell sound asleep. I simply went dead asleep for several hours and when I woke up about four in the morning there was a doctor in the room and he said I'd been drugged with some stuff called Somnolin that he used to prescribe sometimes for Maria Constoupolis. There was an empty bottle of it beside me in the sitting-room where he'd found me when he came to the house, and what's even more extraordinary, he'd found a letter there which was supposed to come from me which said I was killing myself because a love-affair I'd had with some-one at home had gone wrong. Of course it was a forgery, but there was something very peculiar about it. Whoever had written it knew about Hamish and me, and though I'd told Ian about all that in one of my letters to him, I couldn't really imagine him telling anyone else about it."

"Can't you?" Pete said softly. "I can."

"Why should he?" Rachel said. "Who'd be interested?"

"Just a minute," Andrew said. "You said when you woke up there was a doctor in the room. How did he get there?"

"That's another odd bit about the story," Rachel said. "He said someone had called him up and told him there was a woman dying at twenty-one Bessborough Street. Just that, then whoever it was rang off. It was so quick he wasn't even sure if it was a man or a woman. So he'd come along and got in by the back door, which I hadn't locked, and he and his mother, who'd come with him, found me and put me to bed and waited for me to wake up. And a complication was that he didn't know what to believe.

Had I really tried to commit suicide and misjudged the dose of Somnolin, or was I just trying to get attention by taking a quite harmless dose and writing the letter, then ringing him up myself? I *think* by now I've convinced him that I didn't do either, but I'm not absolutely sure of it."

"But if you didn't do either," Sara exclaimed in a shocked voice, "then it can only mean one thing. Someone tried to murder you. Oh no, you can't mean that."

"Well, he nearly murdered me too while he was at it," Pete observed. "I had two drinks from the bottle and I spent the night being sick. It wasn't my take-away foods that did it, Sara darling, it was the wine left so invitingly on the table for Rachel."

Sara shook her head. "It all seems quite impossible. And I'll tell you one of the oddest things about it, though perhaps it's only a small thing. If you're used to taking sleeping-pills, as I suppose Mrs. Constoupolis was and I am, and you go away anywhere, the first thing you think of packing are those pills. You're so scared of being caught without them when you need them that they go straight into your handbag as soon as you begin. I suppose it *was* the Constoupolises who put the Somnolin in the wine, though I can't think why they should have done such a thing. I mean, Rachel was a stranger to them. They can't have had anything against her."

"I don't believe for a moment it was the Constoupolises," Pete said. "I think you need to look nearer home than that."

Eudora stirred in her chair. "If you mean Ian—"

"I don't," Pete said. "And you know I don't."

They stared at one another and for the first time Rachel recognized that there was acute antagonism between them.

"Now wait a minute," Andrew said again, seeming to find it difficult to keep up with the speed of the discussion and constantly wanting them to slow down. "Where have the Constoupolises gone to?"

"Athens," Rachel said.

"Why?"

"Sergeant Ross, who came to see me a little while ago, said they were bolting because they were frightened," she answered. "They've been mixed up in the drug traffic in Adelaide and they were going to talk to the police, and then Ian was abducted, and the police think that was because someone who'd been given the job of picking Alex up went by a verbal description of him that he'd been given and took Ian by mistake. They aren't really in the least alike, but when you say of one of them that he's short and slim and dark and has aquiline features, and you see someone like that come out of the house you've been watching, you could easily get muddled up. I don't know if it's true that that's what happened, but it's what the police think at present."

"I see," Andrew said thoughtfully. "I see. And this man Slattery—you think he's involved in all this."

"It does seem possible, doesn't it?" Rachel said.

"And he's a friend of our neighbours, the Pringles. That's very interesting."

"But he couldn't have put the Somnolin in the wine, could he, or am I just being stupid?" Sara said.

Rachel shook her head. "He couldn't have done it while I was with him and I stayed with him all the time he was in the house. He read the note Alex had left for me, but he never touched the bottle."

"Then it's fairly clear who did that," Pete said. He looked at his father with a trace of amusement, almost of mockery, in his eyes. "Don't you get it, Andy?"

Sara stood up abruptly. There was a slight flush on her cheek-bones. She looked very upset. Finishing her orange juice at a gulp, she said, "Come along, let's eat. I don't like sitting here, making wild guesses. If those people next

door are somehow mixed up with drugs it doesn't altogether surprise me. I've never liked them. And one night,
when I couldn't sleep, I came in here and was looking out
of the window and I saw a catamaran draw up right opposite their home. There was a bright moon, so I saw it
clearly. I don't think they've a catamaran themselves, and
it was a queer hour for anyone to come visiting. I didn't
think about drugs or anything like that at the time, of
course, but after what Rachel's told us, it does seem just
possible that that's what it was. Now please come and
carve the chicken, Andy."

They all moved towards the table and Andrew began to
carve the chicken. But as he began he gave a little chuckle.

"I told you, didn't I, Rachel, that if you wanted to get in
here from the sea a catamaran would be the best thing?"
he said. "So perhaps we've stumbled on one of the routes
by which drugs have been getting into the country. Just up
the Coorong and through the hand-worked barrage to the
south of the island, where no one will see you pass, and so
on till you can hand it over to our friends next door."

"All the same," Pete said as he sat down at the table,
"none of that explains why there was a drug in Rachel's
wine. For that there's got to be a different motive that has
nothing to do with drugs."

His mother was handing the bowl of salad round. Rachel
noticed that her hands were trembling, though her voice
was calm.

"If I were you, I'd leave it to the police to sort that out,"
she said.

With some bewilderment it struck Rachel that Sara was
determined that the question of who might have poisoned
the wine was not to be discussed.

Pete, however, seemed equally determined that it
should be.

"To begin with the motive," he said, "who wanted Rachel dead?"

"Nobody," Sara said. "She's only just arrived. The thing must have been some kind of extraordinary accident."

"It can't have been by accident that someone planted a forged suicide note beside what ought to have been Rachel's body," Pete said. "That was deliberate and cunning, even if it didn't come off." He swung round on Eudora. "For God's sake, Eudora, why don't you tell us how you did it?"

The girl gave a start.

"Are you raving?" she asked contemptuously. "I don't know a damn thing about it." But her vivid, beautiful face had turned an angry red.

"Aren't you the only person, apart from Ian, who's got a motive?" Pete said. There was still a sound of mockery in his voice, as if he thought what a fool the girl was. "Rachel's come into money, hasn't she, and who's she going to leave it to but Ian? And who's going to marry Ian? Don't we all know that? And who would be even happier about marrying Ian than she is already if it turned out he'd a few hundred thousand dollars coming to him? Whether or not he's in the game I don't know. He disappeared just in time to give himself an alibi. But it isn't specially important whether he is or not. What's important is who got at the bottle of wine and when. And who might Ian have shown the letter from his sister to which told him she'd come into a lot of money, and who might have been able to keep that letter so that she could forge the writing for a suicide note?"

There was the sound of a resounding slap as Andrew struck his son violently across the face.

"Shut your mouth!" he yelled. "All right, you've got it in for Eudora, but you aren't going to say that sort of thing about her here in my house!"

"But look at her," Pete said softly. He fingered the mark that his father's blow had left on his face. "Rose-red a moment ago and now snow-white. Why? Could it just be fear?"

Eudora stood up. Her face was indeed very pale.

"It isn't true," she said in a shaky voice. "Not a word of it is true."

"Of course it isn't, Eudora dear," Sara said. "Sit down and have a little more salad. There's some avocado in it if you dig for it."

The girl did not sit down. It was not at Pete that she was looking, but at Andrew.

"I'm not even going to marry Ian," she said. "I told you so."

"I know," Andrew said. For a moment something seemed to leap between him and the girl, a sudden bright gleam of intimacy.

"I don't know how Pete got the idea," she went on. "I never even thought of it."

"Not even when you found out he might have all that nice money coming to him?" Pete said.

His father turned on him again. "You can get out of the house, Pete. No one's going to talk to Eudora like that while I'm here."

"Please, please," Sara said, "I'm sure he didn't mean it. He only meant it's one of the things the police may think and perhaps Eudora should be warned about it."

"I meant every word of it," Pete said.

"It's all right, I'm going." Eudora had recovered her composure, but with it a shrill note had come back into her voice. Her eyes sparkled with anger. "I've never done Pete any harm except to say that I think his bloody writing's a phoney gag. He hasn't any talent. He'll never get anywhere with it. But it gives him a reason for lounging around doing nothing, and if the dole is really all he's living on, I'd be surprised. Ask Sara where some of her housekeeping money goes to."

"That isn't true," Sara cried. She sounded close to tears.

"He'll never take anything from me. Now do sit down, Eudora dear—"

"Thank you, I'm going," the girl said. For a moment she gave Rachel a bright, satirical smile. "Have a happy visit in Australia, Rachel. I hope you enjoy yourself."

Tense with fury, she went quickly to the door.

Andrew pushed his chair back and got to his feet to follow her, but by the time he reached the door, she had gone. He stood uncertainly in the doorway, looking out, till the sound of a car started up in the garage beside the house, then was driven off.

Coming back to the table, he attacked the food on his plate with a look of ferocity, as if he were punishing it for some harm that it had done him.

"Oh dear, what a pity," Sara said. "I do so like Eudora and I thought we were going to have such a nice holiday."

She looked very forlorn.

"But she was right, wasn't she?" Andrew said, putting his knife and fork down with a clatter. He gave his son a look of burning anger. "You don't just live on the dole, do you, Pete? You've a nice little income from other sources, haven't you? I've suspected it for some time. I've guessed why you sometimes come to see us here, though you'll never come near us in Adelaide. I've seen that catamaran come to the Pringles' house and I've seen you go down to the water's edge to meet it. I was pretty sure it was drugs when I saw you bringing a package back with you and I'd have gone straight to the police about it if I didn't know that it would break your mother's heart."

"A lot you care about breaking her heart," Pete said in a soft, bitter voice. "You, of all people!"

"I don't understand what you're talking about," Sara said. "What's the matter with my heart?"

"You see?" Pete said. "She'll cover up for you whatever you do. God knows why, but the poor woman loves you. I believe she'd stand anything from you."

"From you too, I expect you believe," Andrew snarled back at him. "Listen, Sara, how do you like this? This dear son of ours, who's going to electrify the world one day with his genius, isn't just living on the dole, which is a fairly innocent thing to do, even if he's only doing it to avoid a real job of work, but he's deep in with a dirty, squalid drug-smuggling crowd. And that's why he can so nobly refuse your help when you offer him what you can out of the housekeeping money."

If Rachel had had a car, she would have got up and quietly left. But she was dependent on these people to get her back to Adelaide and now was not the moment for drawing attention to herself by saying that she wanted to leave. There was nothing for her to do but sit where she was and watch the scene before her being enacted. It seemed to her that all three Wellmans had forgotten her existence.

Sara looked from her husband to her son, then after a moment helped herself to more salad.

"You must be wrong, Andy," she said. "Pete would never get mixed up in anything like that."

"Wouldn't he!" Andrew said. "Didn't he take to smoking pot when he was a kid of only fifteen?"

"But that's years ago," she said, "and he only did it because the other kids were doing it, as a gesture of independence. It didn't last long. He gave it up almost at once. He told me so himself."

"And you believed him?"

"Of course I believed him. Pete would never lie to me."

"The people who believe that of their nearest and dearest!" Andrew sneered. "They're just the people who tell one the most lies."

"As you've told a few to Sara," Pete suggested.

His father looked as if he were considering striking him again, but instead he grabbed the bottle of white wine before him on the table, refilled his glass and gulped it down.

"Go on," he said. "Tell your mother the truth. You never lie to her, she thinks, so don't lie now. When you were onto pot didn't you get in touch with people who were distributing it and didn't they later suggest to you you might do yourself some good by helping them bring in something a bit harder from the sea? Haven't you been a carrier from our neighbours next door and the Constoupolises? Not difficult for you to do as you'd a perfectly good reason for coming to the island whenever you felt like it. Who was to know you'd never have come near me if you hadn't some pretty good motive that had nothing to do with caring about me?"

Pete said nothing. His face had become peculiarly expressionless.

Sara put her elbows on the table and covered her face with her hands. After a moment, speaking through her fingers, she said, "Is any of this true, Pete?"

He still said nothing.

She let her hands fall and looked him in the face. "Is it true?"

"For Christ's sake, what does it matter if it is or not?" he suddenly shouted. "It's only a small thing. What does matter is that Andy's just found out that Eudora's going to marry Ian for his money and wasn't above trying to murder Rachel to get her hands on it. And that's more than Andy can bear, so he's taking it out on me. He'd make up any story about me for having opened his eyes about her."

"So it's just a story, is it?" she said.

He hesitated, then said, "What else?"

She shook her head. "Drugs!" she said. "Heroin, is it? It's as horrible as murder. It destroys people. Cold-bloodedly destroys them, and all for money. One can sometimes feel almost like forgiving murder, if it's done in hot blood, after fearful provocation. But drugs . . . If it's true you've been handling them, Pete, you must, of course, confess to the police. You must tell them everything you know about those people next door, and the Constoupolises and your own part in it all. I don't know what will happen to you, you'll just have to face that."

"You don't think I'm really going to do that," he said.

"If you don't," she said, "I shall. It's time you grew up and began to realize you've sometimes got to face the consequences of your actions. I know I've protected you because I believed in your talent and that one day you'd become a real writer, and I respected you because you never let me help you. But now I know I've been a fool and should never have listened to you. You should just have had an ordinary job and lived like other people. So, as I said, if you won't confess to the police, I shall have to do it for you."

Pete stood up, looking as if he were about to walk out of the room. But instead he bent over his mother, laying a hand gently on her hair.

"We'll talk about it in the morning," he said. "Perhaps I'll go to the police, if that's what you really want me to do. Meanwhile I'd give a little thought to Eudora, if I were you. In her way that woman is as dangerous as any drug, though I realize I shouldn't have talked about her as I did. That was brutal of me. I'm very sorry."

She sprang to her feet.

"Can't you stop? Can't you be quiet?" she cried. "Can't you see I can't bear any more? Leave me alone!"

"Sara—" her husband began.

She clapped her hands over her ears.

"Be quiet, all of you! I don't want to hear another word from anyone! Be quiet!"

Still with her hands over her ears and her eyes suddenly swimming with tears, she plunged out of the room.

CHAPTER 11

Rachel had never been much addicted to housework, but that evening she was glad that there was washing-up to be done. She, Pete, and Andrew finished their chicken in silence but ignored the cheese and the water-melon until the time came for the table and the sideboard to be cleared and then Pete only put them in the refrigerator, while Andrew disappeared from the room.

Rachel supposed that he had followed Sara and was probably trying to sort out with her the distressing events of the evening. Pete seemed to assume that Rachel would wash up while he helped with the drying, but his help did not run to making any kind of conversation, for which she was grateful. He looked sullen and self-absorbed. A thing of which Rachel was not aware was that she had almost the same look on her small, usually expressive face. She did not want to talk to him, least of all to discuss the scene that she had just witnessed.

She wondered if it was the kind of thing that the Wellmans went in for fairly frequently or if it had been as devastating for them as it had been for her. Other people's quarrels upset her almost as much as those in which, very rarely, she became involved herself. They caused her, if nothing worse, a sense of deep embarrassment. In a way she felt sorry for all of them, because when they had calmed down they were sure to regret having revealed themselves so unguardedly when there was a stranger present.

But were they going to calm down? Was the conflict

actually trivial and would they all have forgotten about it by the morning, or did it go as deep as she had felt at the time that it did?

Whatever the truth was, she determined as she rinsed out the sink and Pete started putting the crockery away that she would somehow get back to Betty Hill in the morning.

She went to her room as soon as the washing-up was finished. She did not go to bed at once, but when she did she soon fell into a restless kind of slumber, made uneasy by dreams. Once more, just as she was about to wake from a short period of sleep, she seemed to hear an enormously loud voice declaiming, "Dilly, dilly, dilly ducks, come and be killed, For you must be stuffed and my customers be filled . . ." It took her a moment, after waking, to convince herself that she had not heard the voice at all, but even when she had done that a question lingered in her mind as to what the customers were to be filled with.

Cannabis, cocaine, heroin?

It seemed, briefly, to be important to find an answer to this, just as it was important, even vitally important, to know if Ian, and perhaps she herself as well, had come half-way around the world to be killed. She could not believe it, yet felt vaguely that she ought not to dismiss the possibility too lightly. With the old nursery rhyme still echoing in her mind, she drifted off to sleep once more.

It was about eight o'clock when she woke again and heard someone moving about in the house, getting breakfast, she supposed, for she could smell coffee. She felt heavy-headed from her disturbed night's rest but got up and had a shower and dressed. When she emerged into the sitting-room she saw Pete at the cooking-stove, busy with a coffee percolator. A door into the garden was open and she saw the two dogs outside.

"Hallo," Pete said. "Sleep well?"

"Yes, thank you," she lied.

"Toast and coffee enough for you, or can't you survive without bacon and eggs?"

"Toast and coffee will be fine."

"That's good, though I do a good bacon and eggs. Living on one's own one has to learn some of the basic things of life."

He sounded cheerful, as if the quarrel of the evening before had left no scars. So perhaps, Rachel thought, the Wellmans were the sort of people who actually were proud of their ability to quarrel and to forget about it within minutes.

Pete brought the coffee and toast to the table, which he had already set with cups and saucers and butter and marmalade. They both sat down and Pete poured out the coffee.

Rachel said, "Pete, I've been thinking, I ought to get back to Bessborough Street today. This morning, if possible."

"You don't like it here?" His tone was light, but his glance at her face was serious.

"Of course I like it, it's just that I can't stop worrying about Ian," she replied. "If he—if he's all right and tries to get in touch with me, that's where he'll expect me to be."

"All right, I'll drive you back this morning," Pete said, readily enough.

"I'm sorry if it's going to spoil your week-end," she said.

"I'd say the week-end is past saving, wouldn't you, after what you listened to last night?"

So he was not going to pretend that the evening before had not happened.

"Do you and your father always quarrel like that?" she asked.

"Usually."

"You really hate one another, don't you?"

"He hates me. I don't believe I hate anyone. It isn't a

writer's job to hate, it's to observe and let one's readers decide how much they hate what one shows them."

"What are you writing, Pete?"

She was very doubtful if he was writing anything at all.

He answered, "My autobiography."

"Isn't it early days for that?" She spread butter and marmalade on her toast. "Don't most of the people who take to writing autobiographies wait until they're in their eighties and have nothing much else to do, and when they look back over the years something starts them thinking what an interesting life they've had and how they ought to be able to write it up and make it interesting to other people?"

"Everyone's had an interesting life," Pete said. "But if you want to get that across to other people you mustn't leave out all the upsetting, human bits, the failures and the humiliations and how you dealt with them, and all the shady things you've done at different times. No, I think I'm at a very good age to get started. I remember my childhood and adolescence very clearly, and isn't that the most interesting time of one's life?"

"I do hope not," Rachel said. "I keep hoping things will get more colourful as time goes on. I don't see why they shouldn't. Actually I think my childhood was pretty drab."

"Oh, so was mine, of course, on the surface. It's what was going on under the surface that I'm trying to bring out. How I've become what I am—why, for instance, I've turned into someone my father hates so intensely."

"And will you write another instalment, so to speak, when you're, say, ten years older?"

"I don't know. I think I might be into fiction by then. Perhaps I'll be mature enough to try it. At present I only feel safe if I anchor my imagination to facts."

But there was always the question, Rachel thought, of how a few years in prison for smuggling drugs might affect him. Then she caught herself looking into his face more searchingly than usual, because she found it very difficult to believe that someone whose expression had such a gentle serenity could really be a criminal.

But was it really serenity, or just emptiness? Serenity might come from the absence of a conscience. A conscience, on the whole, can be a troublesome thing to harbour, very trying to the nerves.

The sitting-room door opened and Andrew Wellman came in.

He had shaved and was in the same shorts and faded blue shirt as yesterday, but there was something different about him this morning. To begin with, as he sat down and helped himself to coffee, Rachel could not decide what it was. Then it struck her that he was in a state of deep abstraction. She and Pete might not have been there. He did not say good morning to her, or ask her how she had slept, or make any of the unimportant remarks that are usually made over breakfast to a visitor. But his presence silenced Pete, who after a moment got up from the table and went to the door that opened into the garden and whistled to the two dogs.

They came up to him, wagging their tails, glad to have an interest taken in them.

Andrew spoke abruptly, "Where's Sara?"

Pete did not answer and Rachel could not have answered the question, even if she had wanted to.

Andrew suddenly pounded the table with his fist and shouted, *"I said, where's Sara?"*

Pete was stroking the dogs and answered without looking round, "In bed, I suppose."

"She isn't," Andrew said.

"Then I suppose she's gone out."

"When? Why?"

"Who knows?"

"Hasn't she been in here?"

"Not since I got up."

The tension between them was working up as before.

"You mean you haven't seen her this morning?" Andrew demanded.

"No." Pete turned back into the room, for the first time looking at his father. "What time did she get up?"

"I don't know," Andrew answered. "I was asleep. Her bed was empty when I woke up and her clothes were gone, so I took for granted she was getting breakfast as usual."

"And I took for granted things were a bit much for her last night and she was sleeping in," Pete said.

"Well, she isn't."

Pete went quickly across the room to the door that led to the bedrooms and Rachel heard one of the doors of the passage beyond it being opened.

Muttering, as if he were speaking more to himself than to her, Andrew said, "What's he looking for? Does he think I can't see when my wife's bed's empty? She must have got up early and gone out."

Pete appeared once more at the doorway into the passage.

"You mean you didn't see these?" he said. He held out both hands.

"What?" Andrew said.

"These, these," Pete said so softly that it was almost a whisper, yet seemed like a shout of fury. He shook his hands in front of his father's face. "An empty bottle of Somnolin. A letter. I haven't read it. It's addressed to you. They were on her dressing-table. Go on, read it. See what you've done to her."

Andrew held out his hand, looking scared and bewildered as Pete thrust the bottle and the letter into it. He gave the bottle a long, uncomprehending look, then put it down and opened the envelope. For a moment he said nothing. His pallor under his tan gave his face an almost yellow look.

Then he said, "No—no, I can't believe it."

"What's she said?" Pete asked.

Andrew held the letter out for him to read for himself. As Pete did so his father covered his face in his hands and gave a violent shudder.

"It's a forgery, of course," Pete said. "She didn't write this."

"She must have," Andrew said, looking up. "Who else could have done it?"

"You!" Pete said.

"Or you!"

They glared at one another with a degree of hatred that Rachel had never seen on human faces before.

Pete turned to her, holding out the letter.

"Look at this," he said. *"You* know that suicide letters can be forged."

She took the letter and read it. It was only a couple of lines.

> I can't go on, Andrew. You know why. Last night was the end of things for me. Sara.

Rachel handed the letter back to Pete.

"But where is she?" he asked of the room. "That's the most important thing to think about at present. She must have taken the Somnolin and written this thing, and then gone away somewhere. But where? Did you really not hear her leave the house, Andy?"

"I didn't hear anything," Andrew said. "As a matter of fact, I'm wondering . . ."

"Yes?" Rachel said as he paused.

"No, I don't suppose it really happened," he said. "But when I went to our room last night, while you and Pete were doing the washing-up, I found her sitting on her bed, crying. And we talked for a time about Pete and what we really ought to do about him and she was taking all the blame on herself for what he's turned into, and it took me some time to calm her down and after a while I suggested we should have a drink and she seemed to like the idea and I got some whisky. She seemed suddenly to have become very peaceful and I'm inclined to believe now that it was because she'd made up her mind what she was going to do. Anyway, we had the drink and went to bed and I went dead asleep. And now I'm wondering if she'd slipped some Somnolin into my drink and that's why I slept so heavily."

"For Christ's sake!" Pete cried violently. "It was you who put Somnolin in her drink. And where is she now? Where did you put her?"

Andrew got up from the table.

"I think I can guess where she may have gone," he said. "If she isn't there, I don't know what's happened to her."

Suddenly in a hurry, he strode to the door and out into the garden. Pete and Rachel followed him.

He was right. Sara lay very peacefully in the boat that was moored at the end of the pathway that led between the densely growing reeds to the river. Except that her eyes were open, she might have been quietly asleep. She was wearing the dress that she had worn the day before, had an arm bent under her head and her ankles crossed. It looked quite normal and reposeful. But her face had the yellow-grey pallor of death.

Pete gave a cry and would have leapt into the boat if Andrew had not grasped him by the arm and pulled him back.

"Don't touch her!" he said. "We mustn't touch anything. We've got to get the police. It's too late to think about a doctor."

"There aren't any police on the island," Pete replied. "That old bloke on the ferry can arrest you if you make trouble on the boat, but he'd be no use here."

"Then it's a case for the Triple O," Andrew said. "They'll

send someone. Meanwhile, take those bloody dogs in-doors."

The dogs had followed them out and were showing a disturbing interest in the boat. Rachel called to them and managed to persuade them to go into the house with her. A minute or two passed, then Pete followed her in, went to the telephone and dialled. She heard him telling someone who answered him that he wanted to report an apparent suicide, then gave his father's name and address.

Putting down the telephone, he went to where Andrew had left the empty bottle of pills and stood looking down at it.

"I've been a fool," Pete said. "I oughtn't to have touched the thing. It's got all our fingerprints on it now, Sara's, Andrew's, and mine. All except yours. And all quite legiti-mately. So it isn't going to help us now."

"Where's Andrew?" Rachel asked.

"Out there with her. Someone's got to stay with her. And there's no harm he can do her now."

"Pete, you don't seriously think he killed her, do you?"

He dropped into a chair, stretched back in it and gazed up at the ceiling without answering.

Rachel waited a little while, then said, "It could really be a suicide, you know. She was very upset last night and my telling her how I'd been doped with Somnolin may have given her the idea of how to do it. Did she often take Somnolin?"

"Every night," Pete said. "She'd a very bad time with insomnia. A doctor we used to have called Rayne first put her onto the stuff, but in those days she only took it occa-sionally. Then more recently another doctor she'd started going to told her to take it every night and used to pre-scribe fairly large quantities at a time. If she'd just got a new lot from him before coming on holiday, the amount she had could have been lethal."

"So don't you think it was probably suicide? The fact

that mine was a fake doesn't mean that hers was. It could have happened as your father thinks. She could have slipped a pill or two into his drink to make him sleep heavily, then written the letter, taken the rest of the pills and gone out to the boat, arranging herself very decently to die in peace."

Pete spoke in a low monotone:

> " 'Till her blood was frozen slowly,
> And her eyes were darkened wholly . . .' "

He went on gazing at the ceiling and Rachel did not try to induce him to speak again.

She thought that he was in a state of shock and she did not feel far off the same state herself. In spite of the warmth of the morning she felt inwardly chilled. The possibility that the tragedy might not have happened if she had not taken it into her head the evening before to talk about her own experience with the drugged wine, something that she would probably not have thought of doing if she had not had the glimpse of Slattery in the Pringles' doorway, and if Pete had not urged her so pressingly to talk, oppressed her distressingly. She did not really think that she was to blame. Whatever had happened in this house in the night would have happened whether she had been here or not. The seeds of it had been sown long beforehand. But having been sucked into the situation, even though it was without knowing what she was getting into, it seemed only natural to feel more involved in it than in fact she was.

Besides, there was something that was puzzling her. Something to do with those two letters. If in fact the second, like the one that she was supposed to have written herself, was a forgery, what did it mean, apart from the fact that that quiet death in the boat was almost certainly murder? It meant something besides that, but what?

She could not find the answer.

It was more than an hour before the police arrived. To Rachel's surprise it was Sergeant Ross who came, attended by a police surgeon, a photographer and three constables. Andrew, who had sat on the path near the boat while he was waiting for them, came into the house, then when the sergeant wanted to talk to him privately, took him into the garden, though not until they had both gone into the bedroom from which Sara had vanished, and Andrew had shown the detective the empty pill bottle and the letter.

It worried Rachel that the sergeant should have come, because it suggested to her that in his view the death of a woman on Hindmarsh Island, a long way from Betty Hill, might somehow be connected with Ian's disappearance and the flight of the Constoupolis couple to Athens. It also presented her with a problem to which she must find the answer before her turn came, as she assumed that it would, to be interviewed by him.

He talked to Andrew for about half an hour, then wanted to talk to Pete, who went out into the garden while Andrew returned to the house. For the first time that morning he seemed to become aware of Rachel's existence. He even managed to give her a painful sort of smile.

"We haven't treated you very well since you arrived in Australia," he said. "I believe if I were you I'd catch the first plane home."

She did not think it was necessary to answer that until Ian, dead or alive, had been found, she had no choice but to remain.

CHAPTER 12

Another half-hour passed before Pete came into the room and told Rachel that Sergeant Ross wanted to speak to her. She went out into the garden and found him seated at a small garden table on which his notebook and a few papers were spread out. He indicated a chair facing him and she sat down. His crooked half-smile appeared on his face as he greeted her, but as usual there was no smile in his eyes.

Before he could begin to question her, she asked, "Have you anything to tell me about my brother, Sergeant?"

"I'm sorry, no," he said. "There are some ideas we're working on but I can't say more than that." He tapped the papers in front of him with a ball-point pen. "Miss Gairdner, I believe there were some things you didn't tell me when I saw you last."

So she had to face the problem that had been disturbing her for so long, whether she wanted to or not. She drew a long breath and let it out slowly.

"Yes, that's something I've been thinking about. I realize I ought to have told you about it, but at the time it didn't seem necessary."

"Are we talking about the same thing?" he asked.

"I believe so," she said. "Isn't it about my having drunk some drugged wine and had a forged letter put beside me, saying that I was committing suicide?"

He nodded. "Yes. I've been told a certain amount about that by Peter Wellman. It seems you talked about it to the family here yesterday evening, and both the Wellmans, father and son, think it may have been what made Mrs.

Wellman think of taking an overdose of Somnolin. But what's puzzling me at the moment is why you didn't tell me the rather strange story about the wine and the letter when I saw you last."

"It was mainly because I was so confused," she said. "It looked as if someone had tried to kill me, and the only person I knew of who had any kind of motive for doing that was my brother. I don't think I've mentioned it, but it happens that some months ago I inherited a fairly large sum of money, and I made a will straight away, leaving everything to Ian. So I thought, if I told you about that, you were certain to suspect him. But I *know* it wouldn't have been him."

"You think, in the normal course of events, brothers don't kill their sisters?" His tone was not unkind, but it had an edge of sarcasm on it.

"I assume it happens from time to time," she said, "just as husbands kill wives and wives husbands and fathers and mothers kill their children and people who have been devoted friends all their lives suddenly go mad and try to destroy each other. But my particular brother wouldn't kill me."

"Then let's go on from there," he said. "Feeling so sure of that, why did you suddenly talk about it yesterday evening?"

"Because of Slattery."

He looked puzzled for a moment, then his face cleared. "Ah yes, the man who forced his way into the house in Bessborough Street to look for the Greeks. But how does he come into things here?"

"Because I saw him here. Mr. Wellman had taken me for a drive around the island and when we were almost home again, just passing the house of their neighbours who I believe are called Pringle, I saw Slattery in their doorway. At least, I'm almost sure it was Slattery. I only saw him for a moment and Mr. Wellman didn't see him at all, but when we got in I explained why I'd been so shocked at seeing him, and then . . ."

She put her elbows on the table and leaned her head on her hands. It was partly because she was trying to remember exactly what had happened then, and partly to avoid his all too perceptive gaze.

"Yes, then?" he said.

"Then Pete Wellman said I hadn't told the whole story and of course I hadn't, so I went on and told them all about the wine and the letter. I don't know if Pete's told you how he came into the story."

"Part of it, at least, but I'd be glad to hear your version of it."

As accurately as she could, she told him everything that had happened the day before after the time when Slattery had forced his way into the house. She told him how she had taken the dogs for a walk, how she had returned to the house to find Pete ringing the bell, how she had taken him inside and told him about Ian being missing, about telephoning Eudora and having a drink with Pete. Then, after he had gone, how the darkness had closed in on her.

"I came to about four in the morning and there was a doctor in the house, a Dr. Rayne, who lives somewhere quite near Bessborough Street," she said. "Mrs. Rayne, his mother, was there too. He told me he'd had a telephone call that there was a woman dying at twenty-one Bessborough Street and how he'd come round and found me. And I wasn't seriously ill at all. But he found a bottle of Somnolin and a letter saying I was killing myself in a conspicuous place. And he began by believing the whole thing was a fake on my part to get attention and it was quite difficult to persuade him that someone else must have put the Somnolin in the wine and forged the letter. But when I told him that Pete had drunk two glasses of the wine he got very excited and dashed to the telephone to ring Pete up and find out what had happened to him. And very fortunately, apparently, Pete had spent the night being sick. I gather that's how that kind of overdose can sometimes hit you. But I think that helped to convince Dr. Rayne that what I'd been telling him was true. Anyway, he took the half-empty bottle of wine away with him to be analysed by a friend of his who's a forensic chemist of some sort."

"So much simpler if he'd left it for us," Ross said with a sigh.

"It was my fault he didn't," Rachel said. "I reminded him that I was his patient and that everything that had happened between us was confidential and that I didn't mean to tell the police what had happened."

He picked up his ball-point again and this time tapped his teeth with it.

"About that drink that you and Pete Wellman had together," he said, "whose idea was it you should have it?"

"Pete's, I think."

"And he poured it out?"

"I believe he did."

"Can you remember exactly what happened?"

"Well, let me think. He suggested we should have a drink and I remembered the bottle of wine in the kitchen and I was going to fetch it when he said he'd do it, and he brought it into the sitting-room with a couple of glasses and poured out drinks for us both. Then he had a second drink himself and then he left."

"But it was he who brought the matter up yesterday evening, getting you to tell the whole story to his parents."

"Yes, but— Oh, listen, Pete couldn't have had anything to do with poisoning the wine or writing the letter. He just isn't like that."

"Have you ever met a murderer, Miss Gairdner?"

She gave him a quick glance, but because of the way that his mouth tilted up at one corner it was difficult to tell whether or not he was serious.

"Not to my knowledge," she admitted.

"Let's leave it at that, then," he said. "Let's agree that anyone who knew you were likely to drink that wine could have drugged it. But let's go back to something else. Let's say Pete could have drugged the wine while he was fetching it from the kitchen, but how did he, or anyone else, for that matter, manage to write that letter? Do you happen to have it with you?"

Rachel opened her handbag, took out the letter and handed it to him.

He read it thoughtfully, then said, "Mind if I keep this? And I'd like a specimen of your writing too. Here—" He handed her his ball-point pen and thrust a sheet of paper towards her. "Just write what it says here. 'Dear Ian—I'm truly sorry about this but I can't face going on. I can't face the loneliness.' That'll do." When she had written it he reached out and took the paper from her and put it and the letter into a wallet that he took from a pocket. "Who's Hamish?"

"A man with whom I had an affair."

"Serious?"

"Oh, very, for a time. Then it died a natural death."

"Your fault or his?"

"It was mutual. I don't believe we ever liked each other so much as after we'd agreed to part."

"And who would have known enough about him to have been able to write that letter?"

"There you are, you see!" she exclaimed. "I knew you'd say that. And I knew you'd leap to the conclusion that it could only have been Ian, and as I've explained, that's why I didn't tell you all this the first time I saw you, because it *wasn't* Ian. But it must have been someone he'd told about Hamish and who'd somehow got hold of one of my letters, so that he or she could have a go at copying my writing. And I find it difficult to imagine him doing that with anyone, but if he did, as I suppose he must have, then I think it could only have been Eudora Linley."

"Ah yes, the missing Miss Linley. Young Wellman has done his best to suggest to me that it was she who poisoned your wine."

"I think it's what he believes. And she had a motive of sorts, I suppose, if it's true that she was going to marry Ian. But last night she herself denied it."

"Would you say . . ." He paused reflectively. "Would you say, just from your own observation of the situation, that there was anything between her and Andrew Wellman?"

"Perhaps there was. I don't know. Pete kept trying to drag it in, but when he did Mrs. Wellman immediately changed the subject, as if she was determined not to be told about it. It was a little as if she felt that what hadn't been said couldn't be true. Then Eudora lost her temper and left, and after that Mr. Wellman turned on Pete and accused him of being mixed up in the traffic in drugs."

Ross nodded. "That's what each of them has been telling me this morning. Pete Wellman claims that his mother must have committed suicide because she couldn't bear the affair between her husband and his secretary, and Andrew Wellman claims that she did it because she couldn't face the truth about her son's criminal activities. Wonderful things, family relationships. Sometimes what I see of them makes me glad I'm an orphan. Now let's go back to Slattery. You're sure you saw him in the doorway of the people next door, the Pringles?"

"Yes."

"And it's more than probable, because of his connection with the Constoupolises, that he's in the drugs business. And Wellman the elder claims that he's seen a catamaran come in to the Pringles' place and that he saw his son taking a package of some sort from someone on board. If any of that is true, the next thing we shall have to do is investigate the Pringles, but meanwhile I want to ask you something about Mrs. Wellman. Was it your impression, when her husband and her son were tearing each other apart, that she believed either of them?"

"I don't know, I really don't know," Rachel answered. "She was terribly upset, but whether that was because she believed either or both, or it was simply because she couldn't endure the way they hated one another, I don't know. In that letter she wrote—"

"Ah, but did she write it?" he interrupted.

She took a moment to digest that, then she said, "You think it's another forged letter? But if you do, you must think . . ."

She stopped and he took her up, "Yes, that her death was murder. Both her husband and her son seem to have had reasons of a kind for getting rid of her. And so, it's possible, had Miss Linley."

"But she wasn't here!"

"No, but she might have prepared a forged letter in advance. Pete Wellman believes it was she who wrote this letter you've given me. He may be wrong. He may have done it himself. The one thing we can be fairly sure of is that his father didn't write it. He's given us an alibi for the last few days which should be easy to check. He drove out here, he says, on Friday, and he and the ferryman greeted each other. It seems they know each other quite well. And he's sure the man will remember his coming and that if he'd left the island later, even for a short time, the man would have noticed it. So that would make it unlikely that he had anything to do with poisoning your wine or forging the letter, apart from the fact that he doesn't seem to have a ghost of a motive for doing it."

"You know, there's something contradictory in this," Rachel said. She could not have said why, but she felt glad that he could not be altogether right. "If Eudora tried to kill me so that she could marry Ian and inherit my money, why should she have helped Mr. Wellman, because I suppose that's what you have in mind, to kill his wife so that she could marry him? It doesn't make sense."

"It doesn't, does it?" he said, giving his twitching little smile again, making her feel that he was pleased with her because she was turning out to be a more apt pupil than he had expected. "So perhaps we're a little further on, since we know something that couldn't have happened. And now what are you planning to do, Miss Gairdner? Stay on here or go home?"

"Home, if you mean Edinburgh," she said, "is rather far away."

"I'm sorry, I meant Betty Hill."

"Well, I was going to ask you about that," she replied. "I'd like to go back there, if I may. Being a complete stranger in the middle of a disaster of the kind that's happened to this family isn't very comfortable. But I haven't a car and unless I can hire one or get Pete to drive me back, I don't know how to get away."

"I don't see why young Wellman shouldn't drive you back," he said. "He can come back here afterwards."

"You don't mind that?"

"I can't see anything against it. We'll know where to get in touch with you if we have any news of your brother."

It struck Rachel that he was even rather anxious for her to leave and perhaps for Pete to take her. She could make no guess why this should be, and naturally she made no mention of her feeling to Pete when she returned to the sitting-room a few minutes later and asked him if he would drive her back to Bessborough Street, assuring him that the police had nothing against his doing this.

The knowledge that they had not seemed to plunge him into deep thoughtfulness and his agreement to drive her to Betty Hill had a reluctant sound about it, but then suddenly he seemed anxious to go and said, "Right, let's get moving."

He drove the Peugeot out of the garage and while Rachel packed the few things that she had brought with her, he waited in the road. When his father heard the sounds of her departure he came out of the room where he had apparently been sitting in order to avoid having to sit in the same one as his son, shook her hand gravely and said he was sorry that she had not had a happier visit. Rachel apologized for having been in the way at such a difficult time, and with the courtesies thus concluded, she collected the dogs, got into the car and Pete drove off.

The day was growing very hot and the sky had taken on the brilliant blue to which she was beginning to grow accustomed. The flat, dried-up, brown fields were peaceful and empty. Pete seemed disinclined to talk, which suited Rachel. She would have liked her mind to become completely blank. It refused to do this, but it did the next best thing. She found herself thinking of the old days with Aunt Christina when one of the only questions that she had ever had to worry about was whether or not she should allow the old woman to have another drink.

Such an important question it had sometimes seemed, when her aunt had been becoming happily, merrily drunk, for after the merriment there could be depression, tears, even anger and a tendency to throw things at Rachel. At times she had been fretted almost beyond endurance by her responsibilities, but how sane and secure those days seemed at this time. She would have given anything to be back in a grey, chill morning and the bitter wind of an Edinburgh January.

"Of course, the police are following us," Pete said absently. "That's why they wanted me to drive you back to Betty Hill. It's to see where I go after I drop you."

Rachel glanced over her shoulder. There was a car there, about two hundred yards behind them.

"And where will you go?" she asked.

"To my room for a while. I need to think."

"But then you'll come back here?"

"I'm told I've got to." He was slowing down. "If they want to follow us, let's make it easy for them. No need to hurry."

The car behind them, a red Vauxhall, suddenly accelerated and went swooping past them.

"Pete, that wasn't the police!" Rachel cried. "It was Slattery!"

"Who?"

"Slattery. The man I told you about."

"Oh, him. Still, look behind you," he said. "There's another car there, isn't there?"

There was, but whether or not it was a police car she could not tell.

"If that's what it is, perhaps it's Slattery they're following, not us," she said.

"If it is, they'll hurry up now to catch him, won't they?"

But the car behind them did not hurry up, nor did Pete speed up once more. When they reached the ferry the barrier had just been lowered and the car in which Rachel had been sure she had seen Slattery was already on the boat, moving away across the narrow strip of water.

She and Pete had to wait till it had made its lumbering progress to the mainland and returned. It did not take long, but Slattery's car was out of sight even before Pete was able to drive onto the ferry.

The car that might or might not have been following them was driven onto it just behind them. With a loud clanking noise the ferry moved back across the river. As Pete drove off it once it had crossed and started the drive towards Adelaide the other car stayed a little behind them all the way to the city, but since this was the main road there would have been nothing particularly strange about this if Pete had not settled down to crawl along at a mere fifty kilometers an hour.

"There, didn't I tell you so?" Pete said after a while.

"They're police, or they'd have passed me long ago. And they don't even mind if I know they're following me."

A thought had crossed Rachel's mind that Pete was driving as slowly as he was not merely to check on whether or not the car behind them was actually following them, but to make sure that Slattery got safely away. She had not yet made up her mind what she believed about Andrew Wellman's accusation that Pete was connected with the drug traffic, but if there was any truth in it, then it probably meant that he had had dealings with Slattery and did not want to let her come face to face with him again. It could also mean that he had some knowledge of what had happened to Ian.

Glancing at his tranquil profile, however, as he drove along the road between the softly folded, tawny-coloured hills, and thinking about the scene that had taken place in the Wellmans' house the evening before, a scene so full of shattering hatred, she felt only uncertainty and confusion. Had she been right that he had no conscience and that that was why he seemed so at peace with himself?

After a while she said, "Pete, about Eudora . . ."

"Yes?" he said.

"Do you really believe she was the person who drugged my bottle of wine and forged the letter about my suicide?"

"If not, who else could have done it? Who else had the motive?"

"But why telephone David Rayne at four o'clock in the morning and tell him I was dying?"

"She could simply have lost her nerve."

"You mean she could have discovered she didn't want to ꞁmit murder."

"˙Well, couldn't she?"

"Do you think your father believed you when you said she'd tried to kill me?"

"I think he did." He was silent for a time. "Yes, I rather think he did."

There was satisfaction in his voice. At the same time he suddenly began to drive faster and Rachel thought that he was not aware of what he was doing, that the urge for speed was merely a nervous reaction to something that was passing through his mind.

They had reached the beginning of the city now and at a crossroads, where the traffic was heavy, a road sign caught Rachel's eye.

It said, "Turn left at any time with care."

At first this struck her as comical, because it seemed to imply that if you did not desire to turn left, no great care was necessary. But after a moment it seemed to be saying something more to her that was not funny at all. It seemed to be saying that if you did not wish to go straight ahead on the beaten track of reasonable virtue, but to turn aside, you should be warned that it was dangerous. Silly, of course, to think about a thing like that. Of course it was dangerous. But virtue had its dangers too.

The car stopped at the gate of 21 Bessborough Street. Both dogs became very excited at recognizing their home.

"Are you coming in?" Rachel asked. She looked over her shoulder as she did so and saw that the car which Pete believed was a police car was still behind them and had also stopped a short distance away.

He shook his head and she thought he was not going to answer. Then he did, but in a way that left her speechless. He put an arm round her and turned her towards him, then as he had done once before, kissed her gently on the cheek.

"Go away," he said. "Keep clear of me. Keep clear of us all."

Then as she got out of the car, he folded his arms on the steering-wheel, bent his head onto them and his shoulders began to shake with what she thought were sobs.

"It's all my fault," he mumbled thickly. "All that's happened. I'm to blame for everything. And I never meant any harm to anyone. I only thought I was being clever. And look what's happened. I'm the one who should kill myself. Yes, for God's sake, keep away from me!"

So she had been wrong that he had no conscience. It was only possible that the one he had had a distorted shape.

Waiting an instant for Rachel and the dogs to be clear of the car, he shot off at speed.

The car that had stopped in the road behind him followed him.

CHAPTER 13

Rachel went into the bungalow, taking the dogs with her. They were delighted to be home again and ran here and there, barking wildly. She realized that they were looking for their owners and when they did not find them a whining sound became mixed with the exuberant noise that they were making. All the same, they had their own priorities. They both reached the kitchen, stayed there and made an even more demanding noise than before.

Rachel went to the kitchen, poured water into their bowl and opened a tin of pet food for them. They lapped up the water and ate the food with relish. She left them to it, went into the sitting-room and dropped into a chair, surprised at how exhausted she felt. But the emptiness of the house was soothing. She had never thought of herself as a person who shrank from human contact as long as it did not come in crowds, and almost for the first time in her experience she discovered that it could be wonderful to be alone.

Looking round the room, she remembered how it and the rest of the house had struck her when she first came into it. It had seemed to her impersonal, hardly lived in, cheaply furnished, temporary, not a real home. It was clean, yet it had given her a sense of not being cared for. At the time she had wondered what had brought Ian here, apart from his desire, of which he had told her, to live close to the sea, and that still puzzled her.

But she understood better now why the place had that temporary feeling. It was quite simply because the Con-

stoupolises had never meant to stay here. They had put
only the most necessary articles of furniture into it, meaning to stay only until they had amassed enough money,
through the distribution of drugs, for a flight to Greece.
Perhaps they had fled earlier than they had originally intended. Ian's disappearance had frightened them. They
had believed that it was Alex Constoupolis who was meant
to have been abducted and they had left before the mistake could be rectified. But to leave soon had always been
their intention.

What would happen to the house now, she wondered?
The dogs, she supposed, would have to be found homes,
but the house was a different kind of problem. It would be
difficult for the Constoupolises to arrange the sale of it
from Athens, since they were now wanted by the police
here and might be extradited if they surfaced. But it could
not be left empty indefinitely, to be taken over by spiders,
rats and snakes, and slowly to start tumbling down.

Of course, if they had rented it, the owner would simply
repossess it. And if they had bought it with a mortgage, the
building society through whom they had bought it would
in time foreclose on it. The Constoupolises would lose a
certain amount of money, but at least they would probably
avoid being either arrested by the police or murdered by
the people who had been their colleagues.

Bungo, the boxer, his appetite assuaged, came into the
room and seemed inclined to be affectionate. As he had
done once before, he tried to climb on to Rachel's lap,
where there was not nearly enough room for him, and
when she gently thrust him back to the floor, he looked
puzzled and hurt. Charlie, indifferent to her, settled down
in a corner of the room and started licking his private
parts. Absent-mindedly she scratched Bungo behind the
ears, wondering why he gave her a feeling which she had
had a few times before that something had happened in

the house during her first morning in it which it would be useful to remember.

It was something to do with the dogs. Something to do with the dogs barking. Something to do with being half asleep and hearing the barking and going to sleep again . . .

Suddenly she knew what it was. She had had coffee with the Constoupolises, then she had had a shower, had gone to bed and to sleep, and then after a time something had wakened her. It had been the dogs barking. And she had assumed that Maria was about to take them for a walk and she had gone to sleep again. But when she got up some time later and found that the Constoupolises had gone, leaving the dogs in the garden, *the gate to the street had been open.*

That simply was not like the Constoupolises. They were fond of their dogs. Probably they had been grieved at having to leave them behind. But they had trusted Rachel to look after them and, though obviously in a great hurry to get away themselves, had taken the trouble to tell her how to feed them. When the Greeks had been leaving they might perhaps have decided that it was better to leave the dogs in the garden, rather than shut up in the house, but they would certainly never have left the gate standing open. It was someone else who had done that.

The barking of the dogs that had wakened Rachel had been caused by someone coming into the house, staying she did not know how long after she had fallen asleep again and doing she did not know what, then being followed out to the garden by the dogs where this intruder had left them with the gate open, so that they could have strayed out into the traffic at any time if they had felt like it. Probably it was only habit that had kept them safely in the garden.

But how had this person got into the house? Had the Constoupolises simply left the back door unlocked or had he somehow got hold of a key? It seemed certain, how-ever, that someone other than the Constoupolises had been in the house that morning while Rachel slept, per-haps had poisoned the wine, perhaps had found one of her letters to Ian and taken it away to copy the handwriting, bringing the forgery back in the night to put beside her drugged body before calling David Rayne to come and look after her.

But apart from the fact that she could not think why anyone should have done such things, there was some-thing here which did not fit. To poison the wine whoever came must have brought some Somnolin with him or her, but why should they have done that? It was true that Maria Constoupolis sometimes took Somnolin and would have had a supply of it in the house, but as Sara Wellman had said, anyone who is dependent on a drug does not leave it behind, even when packing in a hurry. Maria would assuredly have taken her pills with her. So that could only mean that the Somnolin had been brought into the house by the intruder, but probably on a second visit, after he had seen the waiting bottle of wine and had real-ized what he could do. By Pete, for instance.

Rachel gave a little shudder. She thought of his collapse in tears and of his strange confession just before he had driven away, and wondered what it had really meant. He had had access to Somnolin, since his mother took it, and probably still had a key to the Wellmans' home in Ade-laide, even if he hardly ever went there, so that he could have helped himself from her supply. Anyway, since his father had been away on Hindmarsh Island and only his mother had been at home, he might have gone there openly. They had arrived at Bessborough Street together next day, so perhaps he had even been staying with her for once. But that still left the question of motive unanswered. Pete had nothing to gain by murdering her. The only person who just conceivably had was Eudora.

Had he been right that it was she who had drugged the wine?

The telephone rang.

When Rachel answered it, a voice said, "At last. I've been trying to get you again and again all day. This is David Rayne speaking. Have you been away?"

Rachel had thought that there was nothing so necessary to her at the moment as to be alone, but when she heard his voice she realized that there would be one thing better than being alone and that would be to see him.

"I've been to Hindmarsh Island with the Wellmans," she replied. "I've only just got back."

"Nice spot, Hindmarsh Island," he said. "I hope you enjoyed it."

"I can't say I did," she said.

"Something wrong, then?"

"Rather outstandingly wrong."

"About your brother?"

"No, there's still no news of Ian."

"Well, I was going to ask if I could come round to see you. You remember that half-bottle of wine I took away with me; I've got some rather interesting information about it. Can I come round?"

"Oh, do."

"In a few minutes, then."

"Aren't you working?"

"You see, it's Australia Day. I can be got hold of in an emergency, but there aren't likely to be any till the evening when the drunks get loose and walk in front of cars and so on. I've a theory about that wine that I'd like to try out on you. That's to say, it's really my mother's theory. She's a very shrewd woman, with a great understanding of people. Are you alone?"

"Yes."

"Then you might feel like coming out to lunch with us. Anyway, I'll come straight round."

He rang off.

Rachel, putting the telephone down, thought suddenly that it would be a good idea to comb her hair and possibly to touch up her mouth with the lipstick that she had not even remembered that day was in her handbag. It sometimes did you good, she thought, to take the trouble to make yourself presentable.

She attended to these matters and was indeed feeling a little better for having done so when the doorbell rang.

As soon as she opened the door she saw that her attempt to make herself look like her normal self had not been successful, for an expression of concern appeared immediately on David Rayne's long, stern yet friendly face, and he said, "What's the trouble, Rachel? You look as if you've been hit by something very hard and very nasty."

"Yes, it's been difficult," she said.

"Can you tell me about it?"

"I'd like to."

She took him into the sitting-room and as they sat down she found that he was watching her with the kind of masked anxiety that he might have shown if he thought that she was about to describe the symptoms of a disease which could turn out to be fatal.

"Mrs. Wellman died last night," she said. "It looks as if she took an overdose of Somnolin and she left a letter behind. It could be suicide or it just could be murder."

"The same thing all over again, only this time it was successful."

"That's how it looks."

"Suppose we start at the beginning," he said. "Tell me why you went to Hindmarsh Island and what happened there. Then we'll see if we can sort anything out."

She frowned, wondering where to begin, then started a description of how Sara Wellman and Pete had come to see her the day before and had invited her to go out to the Wellmans' house on the island with them. Then she told him how Sergeant Ross had arrived with the information that the Constoupolises had not left for Mildura but for Athens.

By then she was talking fast. The rest of her story, the drive around the island with Andrew Wellman and his description of how a boat could get there from the sea, her glimpse of Slattery, the quarrel between Pete and his father and Eudora's angry departure, followed quickly.

It was when she had to describe the discovery of Sara Wellman's body in the boat the next morning that she faltered, but David Rayne did not help her with questions. He sat listening to her intently, his hands folded, his long legs stretched out before him with his ankles crossed, and with a critical look in his eyes. He would not have been an easy person to delude, she thought, if it had happened that that was what she wanted to do. In fact, it was the opposite. She was telling the story to herself as much as to him and was trying her very hardest to keep it accurate.

She began choosing her words carefully now, but bit by bit unfolded the whole story, the discovery of Sara's dead body, the empty bottle of Somnolin and the letter, the call to the police and the arrival of Sergeant Ross. She told David Rayne all that she could remember of her interview with the sergeant, her drive back to Betty Hill with Pete, the second glimpse of Slattery as he overtook them on the road to the ferry and then the appearance behind them of the car that had stayed on their tail all the way to Bessborough Street and which Pete, no doubt correctly, had insisted was a police car.

"But something very odd happened when we got here," she said. "Pete suddenly burst into tears and began confessing—no, it wasn't exactly a confession of anything, it was more a self-accusation. That's a bit different, isn't it? He said that everything that had happened was his fault, but that he hadn't meant any harm to anyone, he'd only thought he was being clever, but that he was the one who should kill himself. Then he drove off as fast as he could and the other car followed him."

"That kind of confession doesn't always mean much," David said. "Some people, when they're caught up in a calamity, almost like to blame themselves for it. It can be exhibitionism, I suppose, or anyway a kind of egotism. He didn't actually accuse himself of having killed his mother, did he?"

"No, and I'm absolutely sure he couldn't have done that," Rachel said. "He really loved her, I haven't any doubt of it."

"You don't think he'd have done it even to stop her going to the police to tell them about his dealing in drugs?"

She shook her head.

"But do you really think he was involved in bringing drugs into Adelaide?"

She made a gesture of uncertainty. "I don't know. He seems so innocent. But that might be just why he could do it. I mean, perhaps he really didn't understand the seriousness of what he was doing and felt innocent. And then today, after his mother's death, the meaning of it suddenly hit him and he broke down. Though I'm quite sure he didn't kill her, he may have been blaming himself for her death."

"He's sure it was suicide, then, and her discovery of what he was doing was the cause of it?"

"I think so."

"But you yourself aren't at all sure she killed herself."

"I don't know what I think. It's just that it's so like what happened to me. Do you think that could have been— well, a kind of rehearsal?"

He looked surprised. "I hadn't thought of that. I've another idea in my mind that I want to tell you about, but a rehearsal—well, it's an interesting thought. You think someone might have doped that wine experimentally, to see how strong a dose was needed to knock you out? And left that suicide letter behind in case he actually did finish you off?"

"You don't think much of the idea," she said.

"I don't think it fits, somehow. But I've something interesting to tell you about the wine."

"Oh yes, you said so, didn't you?"

"Well, there was no Somnolin in it. It was quite harmless."

"But where did the Somnolin come from then, because something knocked me flat?"

"I think it was in the glass you had your drink out of, before the wine was poured into it."

"But in that case . . ."

"Yes?"

"Only Pete could have put it there."

"Of course."

She stared at him. "But why—why on earth should Pete have wanted to kill me. We'd never even met before."

"He didn't want to kill you."

"But the letter! If he poisoned me, he must have expected me to die, or the letter wouldn't have made sense."

"As it didn't. And you're forgetting the telephone call to me in the night."

"You mean he lost his nerve and found he didn't want to commit murder? That's what he said had happened to Eudora, when he was trying to persuade me she'd put the drug in the wine."

"It could have been like that. But to tell you my mother's idea about the situation, and remember she's a very shrewd woman, it could have been that he wanted to make sure that someone found and read that letter and that you didn't simply destroy it."

"And when you telephoned him and he said he'd been sick over and over again, that wasn't true?"

"Pure fiction. As I said, the wine in the bottle was quite harmless."

She sighed. "I just don't understand."

He fell silent, looking as if he were finding difficulty in choosing the right words in which to express what was in his mind. Then he stood up and started to wander about the room.

"Look, this is only an idea my mother suggested to me after I discovered that the wine in the bottle couldn't possibly have harmed you," he said. "I'm a bit confused about it myself, but I'll make it as plain as I can. It's that the whole thing was a fake from beginning to end and it was intended to be recognized as one. That letter was *intended* to be recognized as a forgery. It must have been, because as there wasn't any serious attempt to kill you it was certain that when you woke up you'd deny ever having written it. Which you did, as you'll remember. Just as he wanted. I think that's got to be the explanation of the letter."

"It doesn't explain very much. It doesn't explain why Pete should have done such an extraordinary thing."

"Didn't you tell me he did his best to persuade you and his parents that Eudora was responsible for the whole affair?"

"Yes, he did."

"Well then, wasn't the whole thing staged to incriminate Eudora? He wanted his parents, particularly his father, to believe that Eudora was a would-be murderess who was going to marry Ian and was after his money. It's looked all along, hasn't it, as if she was the only person who could have any motive for getting rid of you. And it was the letter that pointed to that. Of course, if he'd really wanted to murder you, he needn't have written it. If you'd died of an unexplained overdose murder might have been suspected and Eudora's motive might have been considered. But he didn't really want to do you any harm, he only wanted to be sure that it looked as if someone else had. Hence an obviously forged letter and his call to me in the night."

"As I told you," Rachel said, "when he broke down after he brought me back here he said that he hadn't wanted to do anyone any harm, he'd only thought he was being clever. That fits with your idea, I suppose."

"Yes, I think that that very innocent-seeming young man is really a quite clever and devious character. But there's something still puzzling me."

"There are several things puzzling me, but go on," Rachel said.

"When you first saw that letter you said it was in your writing."

"I was still only half awake. Next day I saw it was a fairly crude forgery."

"But it was a forgery of *your* writing. I mean, to have written it, he must have got hold of a specimen of your writing."

"Yes."

"How could he have done that? Would your brother have let him get hold of one of your letters?"

She leaned forward with her elbows on her knees and her head in her hands. It was a moment before she tried to answer him.

Then she said, "If this theory of yours is right, David, I think I can explain that. I think Pete came in on Saturday morning, soon after the Constoupolises had gone and while I was in bed asleep, and the dogs woke me up, barking at him, but I thought it was just that Maria was going to take them for a walk. How he got in I don't know. And he found me and he found the bottle of wine with Alex's note beside it, and suddenly the whole idea came into his head of how he could fake a murder of me and incriminate Eudora. But, as you said, he had to get hold of a letter of mine, so he went looking for one, and he'd have found it easily enough in Ian's room, because he's one of the people who never throw letters away. I expect, if you look there, you'll find a whole drawer full of the ones I wrote him. So Pete could have taken one away with him and gone to his parents' home to get hold of some Somnolin. His father was on Hindmarsh Island then, so he wouldn't have been afraid of running into him. And then I expect Pete went to his own room and prepared the forgery and then came to see me later." She raised her head. "This isn't just guesswork. I know someone was in the house while I was sleeping that morning because later I found the dogs in the garden with the gate to the street open, and I know the Constoupolises would never have left things like that."

He nodded, returned to his chair and seemed about to sit down when instead he said, "Have you had any lunch?"

"No," Rachel answered.

He looked at his watch. "It's a bit late, but we might go out and manage to get something. The crowds here will be fearful today because of the holiday, but perhaps we'll find somewhere where we can get a meal of some sort. Shall we do that?"

She stood up. "All right, let's try it."

"Do we need to take the dogs?"

"I shouldn't think so. We can leave them in the house. We shan't be gone for very long, shall we?"

"I imagine not."

They set out together.

CHAPTER 14

As David Rayne had warned her, the streets were densely crowded. In the main street where there were several small restaurants as well as tables set out on the pavements under brightly coloured umbrellas, they could hardly move. David took her by the arm to prevent their being separated. All the tables on the pavements had been taken and when they looked into the shadowy depths of the restaurants and cafés they passed, it seemed that there was little hope of finding an empty table. The crowds were a casual and good-humoured lot, dressed in anything from T-shirt and jeans to what was near-nakedness. Faces and bare bodies were scorched red by the sun.

Passing one of the small restaurants, they saw that a couple were just leaving and that their table had been left empty. They went in quickly and sat down, just in time to get ahead of another couple who were trying to jostle their way to it. A damp, sweating waitress took their order of fish and chips. There seemed to be little else on the menu. They had a carafe of white wine which had not much flavour but was cool and refreshing.

Sipping it, Rachel remarked, "You know, when I drank that wine with Pete, I thought it had a curious taste, but I thought that was simply because it was Australian and I wasn't used to it. But I suppose it was really because of the Somnolin in it."

"I should think so," David said. "Some of our wines are pretty good."

"But how did he manage to put the Somnolin into it?

Wouldn't he have had to crush the tablets before he did that? When would he have had time for it? He wasn't long alone in the kitchen."

"If we're right that he came here with a letter prepared to leave beside you later in the evening, he'd also have been able to crush some tablets into powder before he came. Anyway, they dissolve very quickly in liquid. He made a mistake, not putting some into the bottle, but I suppose in the sort of situation he was in you can't think of everything. If there'd been some in the bottle, things wouldn't point so directly at him. He could have been another victim, as he made himself out to be when I telephoned."

"And he must have come back sometime in the night to leave the letter, mustn't he?"

"Yes. But what are you going to do about it, Rachel? Have you thought about that?"

"Not really. I'm still in too much of a muddle about it all. Do you really think we're right, David? You really believe Pete did all this?"

"Can you think of any better explanation?"

"I wish I could."

. "You like him quite a lot, don't you?"

"I did at first. His being a friend of Ian's was part of it. Now I'm not sure."

"Because he's probably mixed up in this dope racket?"

She sighed, idly fingering the stem of her glass. "It's a kind of thing I've never run into before. I've never had to think about anything like it. Do you think he's an addict himself? I mean, if he's hooked on it and can't get off it, it would be a sort of excuse, wouldn't it?"

"When I've seen him now and then, as I have in recent times, he hasn't given me the impression of being an addict. He's struck me as being a very healthy young man. Physically, at least. Mentally it might be another matter. His refusal to take a job and his sticking to his writing—

well, who knows? Perhaps in another twenty years or so
we'll have another Australian Nobel Prize winner, or perhaps it's all pretension and moonshine."

"Suppose it was really he who came in the house on
Saturday morning while I was asleep . . ."

"Well?"

"I wonder, did he know Ian was missing, or did he come
to see him?"

The fish and chips had arrived and as Rachel began on
hers it startled her to realize how hungry she was. The fish
was one that she had never eaten before, some purely
Australian fish, she supposed, though it tasted rather like
haddock.

David did not reply for a moment, then he said, "If he's
breaking down, we may get the answers to all those questions in time."

"You said he wanted to persuade his parents, particularly his father, that Eudora was a would-be murderess.
Why particularly his father?"

He met her eyes with one of his grave stares.

"Isn't his father in love with her? And didn't Pete want
to put an end to that for the sake of his mother? That's the
impression I got from the story you told me about everything that happened out on Hindmarsh Island. You gave
me the feeling that Pete would do anything for his mother,
and when that somehow went disturbingly wrong, he
started coming apart. The plot to destroy Eudora didn't
work out as he expected. Meanwhile, let's go back to that
question I asked you a moment ago. What are you going to
do?"

"There's nothing for me to do except wait till the police
get some news of Ian," she answered.

"But are you going to stay in that house by yourself?"

"I haven't really thought about it. I could go to a hotel, I
suppose."

"I was to give you a message from my mother," he said.

"She thinks you might prefer to come and stay with her. She's got plenty of room as I'll be away, and she likes looking after people."

"You'll be away?" Rachel said with dismay in her voice and feeling a sharp pang of disappointment. She had been letting herself come to feel that he would be there for her to lean on whenever she wanted him.

Perhaps he heard the sound of it, for he gave her one of the smiles that made such a difference to his face and said, "I've been meaning to go, but perhaps I could change it around if you thought I might be useful. It's just that I've got some leave due to me and I was going to Tasmania for a fortnight, for some trout-fishing. You ought to go to Tasmania yourself sometime before you go home. It's very beautiful. Something like the Scottish Highlands, except that it's got trees and a blue sky over it."

"Do you know the Highlands, then?" she asked, surprised.

"I've driven around in them a certain amount. I did a year of my medical training in Edinburgh. And I explored the Highlands a bit. I even came on a village on the northernmost coast of Sutherland called Betty Hill. Have you noticed we've a way of naming places here after places in Scotland? You're from Edinburgh, aren't you?"

"I lived there for about ten years with an old aunt after my parents—that is, my mother and my stepfather—were killed in a car crash. Aunt Christina appeared on the scene then and looked after Ian and me. And I went to Edinburgh University and then started teaching in a school there, but Ian went to the London School of Economics and then got a job with Ledyard Groome. I suppose when you were in Edinburgh I must have been there too. We might have met."

"I wish we had. Only you'd have been quite a young thing and I'd have been far too old to interest you."

She laughed. "I don't know about that. I don't think you're so very much older than I am."

"D'you know, I think that's the first time I've heard you laugh," he said. "I like it."

"I'm afraid the circumstances of my visit haven't been exactly conducive to hilarity," she said.

It was he who laughed now. "What fine, well-rounded periods you sometimes use. Is that the Scot in you? I noticed when I was there that they had a liking for polysyllables. But you haven't answered my question. Wouldn't you like to move in with my mother? Both she and I hate the thought of you staying in that house alone."

"It's very kind of her. I'd like to. Only I'm not sure . . . You see, it's because of Ian. Suppose he comes back and finds I'm not there. The thought of that worried me when I went to Hindmarsh Island."

The smile faded from his face and it acquired once more the look that was almost severe. But there was doubt in his eyes. All at once she was quite sure that she knew what was passing through his mind.

"You think he won't come back, don't you?" she said.

"It's a possibility you'll have to consider sometime," he replied.

"I know, I'm not quite stupid. And the police have told me so."

"And you're going to sit it out by yourself in that house?"

"Oh, I'll have the dogs," she said.

The forced note of flippancy in her voice seemed to irritate him.

"We've got to look after you, don't you see?" he said. "And you aren't making it easy for us. Now why won't you come and spend a few nights with us? It would be far the best thing to do. And I'll go to Tasmania or stay behind, whichever will help you most."

"You're so good, David. I wish I could tell you properly how grateful I am."

"But you won't come."

"May I think it over? If we go back to the house now I could telephone the police again and see if they've any ideas about the matter."

"And you could pack a suitcase and we could go round to the flat straight away."

"You do stick to a subject once you're on it, don't you?" she said. "Very well, I'll come. And thank you. Thank you so much."

They got up, David paid the bill and they went out on to the pavement, thrusting their way again through the dense crowd.

They went back to Bessborough Street along the Esplanade, the road above the beach. As it had when Rachel had last walked along it, it struck her as some crazy kind of refugee camp. There seemed to be even more tents on the beach and on the strip of grass above it than there had been before. Their colours were brilliant and music issued from nearly all of them, wildly discordant, because all the radios were tuned in to different stations. Children wandered about among the tents, some enthusiastically throwing balls, some too small for that, staggering about on fat, immature legs and occasionally falling flat on their faces, some crying piteously as if the world were too much for them to cope with. The edge of the sea, where only the smallest of waves were toppling over and spreading across the sand, was a seething mass of people. As she had thought before, it was like a grotesque caricature of the kind of scenes in drought-stricken parts of Africa with which television had made everyone familiar.

Rachel wondered if you might think of all these healthy-looking and energetic people as refugees of a sort. Refugees from work, from responsibility, from habit and dullness. And did the custom of taking a holiday at least once a year go back to something very primitive in the human being, who had once been a nomad, living in tents, driving his flocks before him rather than settling down to the routine of agriculture, and picking up take-away food whenever he found it in convenient spots in the desert?

It was only very rarely, she thought, that you encountered a person who actually disliked and avoided going on holiday, even if, when many of them did so, they knew it was their tendency to pick up some strange infection and to have to spend half the time that they were away from the security of their homes living on antibiotics and hoping that their stomachs would soon settle themselves. On their arrival home they would all swear that they had had a wonderful time, and in a sense it probably would have been wonderful, since it would have achieved the miracle of making them delighted to see once more their kitchens, their offices, their shops, their laboratories or wherever they happened to work.

Rachel and David did not try to talk as they strolled along slowly through the throng. Ahead of them it looked a little denser than where they were at the moment. A knot of people were gathered around a bench, all absorbed in contemplating someone who was sprawled upon it. It was the same bench where Rachel had sat on her first evening in Betty Hill and where she had first met David's mother. The people standing around it seemed to be arguing.

"Dead drunk, that's all," Rachel heard a man say as she and David came closer.

"That's for sure," another said. "Had a beer too many."

"I tell you, he's ill," a woman said. "We ought to get an ambulance."

"You don't get an ambulance for a drunk," the first man said. "He wouldn't thank you for it. Poor chap, you leave him in peace and give him a chance to sleep it off."

"I tell you, he's ill," the woman insisted. "You don't go that colour when you're drunk."

"Could be you're right," someone else said. "Could be we ought to get a doctor."

"Drunk," a new voice said. "Didn't you see how he staggered when he got out of the car? Just a beer too many, as my mate said. Far the best to leave him."

Rachel began to run.

She had only a few yards to go and plunging through the group gathered around the bench, she caught the sprawling figure in her arms.

"Ian!" she cried, her voice breaking as tears began to choke it. "Ian!"

David came up quickly behind her.

"It's Ian?" he said.

"Yes, yes, yes!"

She held him to her almost as if he were a child. His black hair, usually so smooth, was tousled and there was a sour smell about his body, as if he had not washed for days, or perhaps had vomited over himself. He was wearing a soiled white shirt and dark trousers.

"You know him, dear?" asked the woman who had insisted that Ian was ill.

"Yes, he's my brother," Rachel said. "We've been looking for him . . ." She looked up at David. "He *is* ill. They've done something to him."

He was bending over Ian.

"Drugged, is my guess," he said. "We'd better get him home." He looked at the man who had spoken of Ian staggering out of a car. "You saw him come here?"

"That's right," the man answered. "Saw him get out of a car that slowed down for a moment, seemed all right, then grabbed at this bench and collapsed on it. Passed straight out."

"What kind of car?" David asked.

"A red Vauxhall."

"Did you see the driver?"

"Can't say I did. I was looking at this bloke, wondering if he was all right."

"It doesn't matter, I know it was Slattery," Rachel said. "A red Vauxhall—that's what he was driving when he passed Pete and me before we got to the ferry. Perhaps he'd got Ian in the car with him then. But what are we going to do now, David?"

"The easiest thing would be to get him up to our flat," he said, glancing up at the big block of flats behind them. "There's a lift. I wonder if he can walk at all."

"Want any help?" the man who had been certain of Ian's drunkenness asked.

"Thank you," David said. "Yes, we could do with that. Ian . . ." He bent over Ian again. "Can you walk a little way?"

Ian grunted and opened dazed eyes for a moment, then quickly closed them again as if the sunlight were too much for him.

"Rachel," he mumbled.

"Yes, I'm here," she answered.

"Got to get to the airport to meet her," he said in a slurred, drowsy voice. "I told them that. Got no time to spare."

"Never mind about that," David said. "The clever girl got here all by herself."

He slid an arm round Ian. Between them, David and the man who had offered assistance got him on to his feet. With both of them to support him it seemed that he could stand, though his head lolled forward onto his chest. The crowd around the bench began to melt away. David and the other man helped Ian slowly forward, almost carrying him, with Rachel following anxiously behind them. They reached the entrance to the block of flats and crossed the foyer to the lift.

As the three men and Rachel entered it, the kindly stranger said, "Did I hear you say he was drugged?"

He was a big, muscular man with a square head and a brown, good-natured face.

"That may be the trouble," David answered.

"You a doctor, then?"

"Yes."

"Lucky you came along. Is he a patient of yours? One of those registered addicts one hears about?"

"I don't think he's an addict at all."

"Is that right? What happened to him, then? I know he was pushed out of that car."

"That doesn't surprise me," David said. The lift came to a halt and its door opened. "Thank you very much for your help."

"Yes, thank you," Rachel echoed warmly.

"You're welcome." The man turned back into the lift and the door closed on him.

With his arm still round Ian, David supported him to one of the doors in the narrow hall. With his spare hand he fumbled for a key in his pocket and unlocked the door. Ian was beginning to stand more securely and had opened his eyes again, and with only a little help he managed to walk forward into the big, pleasant room into which the door opened, though there was still a look of dazed incomprehension about him.

Mrs. Rayne was in the room, sitting in a chair by a door that opened onto a small balcony. She stood up quickly, giving a little cry of astonishment as she saw them come in.

But she was not alone in the room. Sitting in another chair and not standing up quite as quickly as she did was Sergeant Ross.

CHAPTER 15

David guided Ian to a sofa. He gave a bleary look round, then closed his eyes and seemed inclined to go to sleep again. But suddenly he opened them and gazed at Rachel. She sat down on the sofa beside him and took his hand in hers.

"Most extraordinary," he muttered. "So you got here all right."

"Yes, of course," she said.

"Where are we?"

His face was pale and he could not have shaved for several days. There was a dark shadow all round his jaw. His hair looked not only uncombed but as if it had got dust in it. He had a high-bridged nose and dark, deep-set eyes. What Rachel had said about him to Sergeant Ross was true, yet he had no resemblance whatever to Alex Constoupolis.

"We're in the flat of some friends," she said. "We found you outside and brought you in."

He addressed himself to Mrs. Rayne in the courteous tone that was natural to him. "Very kind of you. I'm sorry I'm being a trouble to you."

"Don't worry about that," she said. "Would you like some coffee?"

"I would—I would indeed," he answered. "But I don't want to be any trouble to anyone. And may I ask who you are? I can't remember ever having been here before. Is that my memory—it seems to have gone a bit blank—or haven't I been here?"

"No, you haven't," she answered, smiling, "though

we're near neighbours. My name's Charlotte Rayne. And this is my son David who brought you in."

She went out to make the coffee.

"And you're Rachel—you're really Rachel," Ian said, gripping her hand hard. "I had an idea I might never see you again. But that's some time ago. I'm not sure when it was." His gaze settled on the face of Sergeant Ross. "And may I ask who you are?"

"I'm Detective Sergeant Ross," the sergeant answered, "and I've been looking for you for the last few days."

"And you found me. Thank you."

"It was your sister and Dr. Rayne who found you."

Ian looked back at David. "I haven't thanked you. I was on a bench, wasn't I, with a lot of people round me? Then Rachel came . . ." He gave a puzzled shake of his head. "I was a terrible fool, you know. I remember that now. I can't think how I ever came to do such a thing, I mean, letting two complete strangers start jostling me in the street and not fighting them off. I can't think how I let it happen, except that I was taken by surprise. But you're being very kind to me."

"Just take it easy," David said. "You'll feel better presently."

"I don't want to be any trouble to anyone," Ian repeated in his firm, punctilious way.

"That's all right, you're welcome," David said. "The main thing is, we've found you. Rachel's been going nearly out of her mind, not knowing what had happened to you."

"There was no way I could let her know," Ian said apologetically. "I didn't even know myself where they were taking me till I heard the clanking noise. I recognized that. It was the noise of the ferry. I've been out to Hindmarsh Island a few times, you see, to visit the Wellmans. Very hospitable people. Very kind to me ever since I got to Australia. So I knew the noise. But may I ask who you are? I mean, Rachel's only just got to Australia, hasn't she? She hadn't any friends here that I know of. So how did you meet her?"

"It's a rather complicated story," David said. "We could save it up for later. But this flat is only just round the corner from Bessborough Street, and it happened I was called in . . . Well, she wasn't well, and when I saw her she told me how you'd gone missing."

Ross said, "That's something I was going to ask you about, Doctor. This morning Miss Gairdner told me how you met—all those things she didn't tell me before about the drugged wine and the forged letter—things she ought to have told me about when I first met her. A pity she didn't. It might have helped, though perhaps it wouldn't really have made much difference. Anyway, I think we know where we are about all that now. But I just want to know if you confirm her story."

"Is that why you're here?" David asked. "I was going to ask you that."

"That, and to ask you about a half-full bottle of wine which you made off with before I got to Bessborough Street," Ross replied. "I'd like to know what's happened to it."

"You can check that with Dr. Melder, of the forensic department of the university. I asked him to analyse it and he's come up with the answer that there's nothing whatever the matter with it."

"No Somnolin in it?"

"No."

"Nor anything else?"

"According to him, it's just a bottle of rather inferior claret."

"That's very interesting."

"It is, isn't it? But perhaps in view of Mr. Gairdner's state, we ought to leave discussion of it until later."

"I'm all right," Ian said quickly. "I'm quite all right. I'm feeling fine." He did not look as if he were feeling fine, though life was returning to his face. "You said something about drugged wine. Did someone give Rachel some drugged wine?"

"Yes, and I'm pretty sure who it was," David said.

"Then please go on." Ian's tone was nervous and urgent. "I'd like to hear about it."

David turned to the sergeant. "You know who it was, of course."

"We've got our theory about it," Ross replied. "But I'd be interested to hear yours."

"It's mostly my mother's, though she hasn't heard all the facts yet. They begin with the fact that Miss Gairdner is almost certain that someone came into the bungalow on Saturday morning, while she was sleeping off her journey. She was wakened by the dogs barking, but went to sleep again. Then later she found them in the garden, but with the gate to the street open, and she was certain the Constoupolises would never have left them like that."

"The dogs!" Ian exclaimed. "I promised to look after them while Alex and Maria were in Mildura. Where are they?"

"Alex and Maria, or the dogs?" David asked.

"Both," Ian said. "Have Alex and Maria got back?"

"They haven't, and to the best of my knowledge, they won't be coming back," Ross said. "They're in Athens."

"But the dogs are all right," David said. "You needn't worry about them. Rachel has been looking after them. Well, Sergeant, my theory is that the person who came into the house was Pete Wellman. I'm not sure why he came. You may know more about that than I do. However, I'll leave that for the moment. I think when he saw Rachel and realized she was sound asleep, he prowled round the house, found the wine and the note that the Constoupolises had left for her, and suddenly he had what he thought was a brilliant idea. He knew, I suppose from her brother, that she'd recently inherited a lot of money, and that if she died, he'd inherit it. So Pete decided to stage an attempted murder of her, because he was sure that the person who'd be suspected of it would be Eudora Linley."

"Eudora?" Ian interrupted agitatedly. "In God's name, why Eudora?"

"Weren't you engaged to her?"

"No—well, no, not exactly. I thought we were for a time, but it was quite a mistake."

"Pete thought you were, however, or on the edge of it. And if you were, she'd a motive for getting rid of Rachel, and she seemed to be the only person who had. Pete himself certainly hadn't, and in fact, you see, he didn't do Rachel any harm. He hunted about till he found some letters of hers in your room and took them away with him so that he could forge a suicide letter, supposed to be written by her. He also went to his parents' house and got hold of some of his mother's Somnolin, then in the afternoon he came to see Rachel and had a drink with her. The drink came out of the bottle of wine the Constoupolises had left, but it was Pete who poured it out, and before handing Rachel her glass, he laced it pretty strongly with Somnolin. Rachel thought it tasted peculiar, but in her innocence she thought that that was just because it was an Australian wine and she was too polite to remark on it. So she drank it and soon she was fast asleep. And sometime that night Pete slipped into the house again, put the suicide letter and an empty bottle of Somnolin beside her, telephoned me to say there was a woman dying at twenty-one Bessborough Street, so that I came hurrying round, and slipped away again. And the real reason he phoned me wasn't because he was afraid Rachel might die and he'd have unintentionally committed murder, but because he wanted to be sure that some detached person would see that letter and that Rachel herself wouldn't have a chance of just tearing it up. And he wanted the letter recognized as a forgery. In other words, he wanted the whole thing to look like a bungled attempt at murder, without, in fact, any damage having been done."

"And what was his motive?" Ross asked, and from something in his voice Rachel thought that he had a fairly clear idea in his own mind of what that motive had been.

"I think it was to persuade his father that the woman he was in love with was a murderess," David replied, "and furthermore, that she had only been stringing him along and had every intention of marrying Ian, anyway if he had enough money. From what Rachel's told me of the evening on Hindmarsh Island, I understand it was Pete who urged her to tell the whole story to the Wellmans. He wanted to put an end to the affair between his father and Eudora, for the sake of his mother, that's all, and what he never thought of was that the whole scheme could misfire and that Andrew Wellman would murder his wife so that he could marry Eudora and be sure of holding on to her."

"That's exactly what Pete Wellman has been telling us," Ross said, "in case that's of any interest to you."

Rachel started forward on the sofa.

"You mean you've arrested Pete!"

"No, no, it's just that he's been talking a lot, in fact won't stop, getting a lot off his chest," Ross said, giving his crooked smile, as if he felt that perhaps he ought to reassure her.

"But when have you seen him?" she asked. "Where did he go when he dropped me off in Bessborough Street? It was your men following us, wasn't it?"

"That's right. We wanted—it's an old trick—we wanted to put a little pressure on him. And he went back to the room he's been living in recently and stayed there for perhaps an hour, and then he drove straight to Police Headquarters."

"He said he wanted some time to think," she said.

"I take it then, that that's what he was doing in his room," Ross said. "Thinking. And the outcome of it was that he told us the whole story of how he thought of doping Miss Gairdner's wine and forging a letter in her name, and getting her to tell the whole story to his parents, so that his father would be put off continuing his affair with Miss Linley. And how it all went wrong and his father accused him of acting as a carrier for some drug pushers, and then how he copied what his son had done, giving his wife a doped drink and forging a letter from her, saying she was killing herself. He hoped, his son thinks, that the blame, if there was any suspicion about her death, would fall on him, and he's been telling us how it was all his own fault because it had turned out that his father could only think of how he could keep Miss Linley and stop her marrying Mr. Gairdner. You've got very near to the truth, Dr. Rayne. I congratulate you."

Mrs. Rayne came into the room with coffee. She started to pour it out.

"I think I heard most of that in the kitchen," she said. "But what about the drugs? Has Pete Wellman confessed he was connected with all that?"

"Not yet," Ross said. "But I think he will in the end, you know. He's no fool, though perhaps a bit simple in some ways. He'll see it's really the best thing for him to do. Mr. Gairdner, can you tell me how you came to take a room with the Constoupolis couple?"

Ian was eagerly gulping down hot coffee. For a moment, at being directly addressed, he looked bewildered, then he said, "Yes, of course, it was Pete who arranged it. We were quite close friends, you know. He didn't work at Ledyard Groome, but he'd a way of drifting into the office and we'd go out and have a drink together, and sometimes I'd go to his room and listen to his records and so on. And I happened to say I wished I could find a room close to the sea, because I'm very fond of swimming and it seemed to me a waste of this wonderful climate not to be able to swim whenever I felt like it. And he said he'd some friends who'd recently taken a house in Betty Hill and how they wanted to let a room, and it wasn't very attractive, but the Constoupolises said they'd only just moved in and would be improving it, and it was only a few minutes' walk from the beach, and it was cheap, and they seemed nice people too. They fed me awfully well. Greek cooking. Wonderful crayfish dishes sometimes. So I'm not sure if I'd have stayed much longer or not, but they had a room they said I could have for Rachel for as long as she wanted to stay, and I promised to look after their dogs while they went to Mildura for the holiday."

"But your friend Pete never said or did anything that made you think he might have a special reason for wanting you to live in the Greeks' house?" Ross said.

Ian thought about it, then shook his head. "He used to visit me quite often there. He'd just drift in, as he did at the office, and stay and talk, and sometimes we'd go for a swim together, and then he'd drift off again. He never seemed to have much to do. He used to talk about writing, but unless he did it late at night I don't know when he actually got down to it. He said he was living on the dole, but he never seemed to be short of money. I assumed his mother was helping him."

"She wasn't," Rachel said. "I heard her say she wished he'd let her."

The sergeant put the tips of his fingers together and contemplated them thoughtfully.

"I'm sure he'll admit he was in the drugs racket in the end," he said. "It all fits together so well. I don't know how he first got into it. For all we know, he may have been in it for years. Some of these types get started in adolescence. But he isn't an addict himself. He may have got to know someone who was, or perhaps who was deep in the thing, for instance the Constoupolises themselves, who saw how useful he could be bringing the stuff in from Hindmarsh Island. That's where it was being landed, we think, though it would have been a dangerous operation getting it in there. It's been done in the past, however, and we think it was coming in by catamaran from a ship out to sea that came perhaps from Indonesia, and was handed over to a couple called Pringle. And because the Wellmans had a house there, Pete had a perfectly innocent reason for going to see them, and once Mr. Gairdner was established in the Constoupolises' house, he'd a quite innocent reason for going there to see his friend. So a package could be picked up and delivered without attracting attention." He gave Ian a long, steady look. "This is all new to you?"

Ian drank some more coffee, frowned and said, "Not exactly. If you'd asked me that a few days ago I'd have said it seemed to me utter nonsense. But now . . . Well, I've had a very peculiar experience and I've got to admit, I suppose, that Pete was involved in it. But I don't much like doing that, because I believe he saved my life."

"When the Pringles took you by mistake, thinking you were Alex Constoupolis?" Ross said.

"Yes, that's what happened," Ian said, "though I couldn't make head or tail of it at first. I went to work as usual on Friday morning, then I went out to lunch and a couple came into the café just after me and sat down at a table near me, and when I left they followed me out. And they started crowding me against a line of cars that were parked there in a way that annoyed me, but I didn't seem able to get away from them, and then suddenly, as we were passing one car—I'm sorry, I'm not very clear about this part, because my memory's a bit blurred—I think they simply knocked me sideways into it and then I blacked out. I suppose they gave me an injection of some sort."

"But you began to come to later and you heard the clanking noise of the ferry," Ross said.

"Yes, but it didn't mean much to me at the time. I thought: That's the ferry; and it made no sense to me, being there. I was in the back of a car and there was a rug over me and I was almost stifled. I must have moved or said something, I'm not sure what, but somehow I attracted the driver's attention and he shouted at me to stay still or he'd finish me off. And the car stopped and the door was opened and the rug was pulled away and I realized I was blindfolded. Except for that clanking noise I'd heard, I'd no idea where I was. And they hauled me out of the car and took me into a house and into a room and they pushed me down on a bed and tied my hands together so that I couldn't get at the blindfold, and left me there. I don't know how long it was. It felt like hours. Then at last the couple came back and I could hear they'd got someone else with them, and he came in and stood over me and after a moment he said, 'You fucking fools, you've got the wrong man!' "

"Slattery!" Rachel exclaimed.

"I shouldn't be surprised," Ross said. "And what I believe had happened was that Slattery and the Pringles had intended to abduct Constoupolis. Word had got round to them, I don't know how, though I'm afraid it may have come from someone in the police force, that Constoupolis was going to talk in return for protection for him and his wife till they could get away to Greece. So Slattery's idea was to silence him, and as he'd never seen the Pringles before, they were chosen for the job. They were given his description, and my guess is it was Pete Wellman who gave it, and they picked up a man who fitted the description when he came out of twenty-one Bessborough Street, followed him and kidnapped him. I'm sure Miss Gairdner will remember, when she gave me your description, that I said it fitted Alex Constoupolis, and it did, although she was quite right when she said there was no resemblance between you."

"What happened, Ian, after Slattery saw you?" Rachel asked.

He looked round at her and gave the first smile that had

appeared on his drawn face since she and David had found him.

"God, it's good to see you again!" he said. "I told you, I thought I never would, and it felt so important to see you at least once more. It's so long since we were last together. Poor old Aunt Christina, I expect you miss her, don't you? She was good to us, wasn't she? Was she drunk or sober when she died?"

"She died in her sleep, so we'll never know for sure," Rachel said. "She looked very serene. But, Ian, about Slattery—"

He made an impatient gesture. "Have we got to go on talking about it? I've told them how I was kidnapped and the sergeant's explained why it happened, so isn't that all that matters? Can't we talk about what we're going to do next?"

"We'll go back to Bessborough Street presently," she said, "and you can have a long rest. But, Ian, did you ever tell Pete I'd inherited a lot of money from Aunt Christina?"

He looked uncertain. "I believe I did. I was very pleased about it. I said you'd been wonderful with the old girl and deserved it."

"And Hamish?" she said. "Did you tell him about Hamish?"

"Who's Hamish?" he asked. Then recollection seemed to come to him. "Oh, of course, Hamish. No, why should I? I never even met the man. None of my business."

"But Pete took your keys of the bungalow from you, didn't he?" she said. "That's how he got in on Saturday morning. It wasn't because the back door had been left unlocked." She turned to Ross. "You see, I think the letter Pete took to copy my suicide letter from must have been the one in which I told my brother how I'd broken off my relationship with the man who was mentioned in the note Pete left beside me. But something I still don't understand is why Pete came to Bessborough Street that Saturday morning. He must have heard by then from Slattery or the Pringles that they'd got the wrong man, and I suppose they knew it was Ian. So why should he have come to the house at all?"

"I think to see Constoupolis," Ross answered. "Whether to warn him what might happen to him if he stuck around or to make sure he stayed there till Slattery turned up, we don't know yet. As I told you, he still isn't admitting having had anything to do with the drugs side of all this, or the Pringles, or Slattery. In any case, Wellman was too late to catch the Constoupolises. They'd understood what had happened and had bolted already."

"And what have you been doing about all these people?" Mrs. Rayne asked. "Have you arrested them?"

"We've taken the Pringles in for questioning, but we haven't charged them yet. Their house has been searched, but we found nothing of interest in it—nothing connected with drugs, that is—and until Pete Wellman decides to talk, we've no firm evidence against them."

"But the murder of Pete's mother—can't you do anything about that?" Mrs. Rayne said. "That is—I suppose it was murder, not suicide."

"No, it was murder," Ross said. "The letter she was supposed to have written was a forgery, just as Miss Gairdner's was."

"You mean Pete did that too?" Rachel said incredulously. "I can't believe it. I can believe all the other things about him. I think he's too—well, undeveloped to have realized how serious the drugs business was. But he really seemed to love his mother. I can't believe he'd murder her."

"I'm sorry, what I said may have been misleading," Ross said. "I said the letter was a forgery, but our expert said at once the two letters were forged by different people. And as it happens, Andrew Wellman has confessed to writing the second letter and to his wife's murder."

"There!" Mrs. Rayne exclaimed, excitement glowing in her old, experienced face. "I was sure of that from the start. So you've arrested him, have you?"

"Well, no," Ross said.

"No?" she said. "Why not?"

"Because he didn't do it," Ross answered.

CHAPTER 16

There was silence in the room, which made Ross stir uneasily in his chair, as if he were finding himself in deeper waters than he had bargained for. He drew a hand down the side of his face and tugged at his chin.

"Perhaps I'm not very good at explaining myself," he said. "He intended to do it sometime, you know, and I think the story Miss Gairdner told him of what happened to her gave him the idea how to do it. His motive was simply that he knew he'd never persuade his wife to divorce him and Miss Linley was demanding marriage. And he told us he and his wife had a drink together before going to bed and hers had a massive dose of Somnolin in it. If she'd drunk it she'd have become unconscious quite soon and he could have got to work, writing the letter. But he couldn't do that at once, as he planned, because he went to sleep himself."

This caused another silence. He frowned with a look of perplexity, as if his own statement bewildered him. He began ticking things off on his fingers.

"Look," he said, "first, we found two empty glasses in the Wellmans' bedroom. There were traces of whisky in each and traces of Somnolin in *both* of them. Don't you see what that means? It means that while Wellman was doping the drink for his wife, she managed to slip some Somnolin into his. And she didn't drink her whisky at all. At a guess, it went down the toilet, because she wasn't feeling in the least like a drink just then. She wanted to stay very wide awake. But she wanted her husband to sleep, which he did. He didn't normally take sleeping-pills, so they hit him hard. Next, she slipped out of the house and went to the Pringles'. We've found her fingerprints on a teacup and on the wooden arms of a chair she must have sat in. She tried to find out from them if there was any truth in her husband's accusation that her son had been handling dope. It was a wildly reckless thing to do, but she doesn't seem to have realized she was dealing with professional criminals who wouldn't hesitate at a little thing like murder. But I suppose she cared about that son of hers as much as he did for her."

"And you mean there was dope of some sort in that tea they gave her?" David asked.

"Oh no, she didn't die of an overdose of anything. We'll have to wait for the autopsy to be sure, but we're fairly certain she was smothered."

"By Slattery!" Rachel cried.

Ross gave a sardonic grin. "You really do seem to have taken a dislike to that man, Miss Gairdner. I wouldn't like to be him if you ever get your hands on him. I don't think he'd have much of a chance. But I wouldn't be surprised if you're right. Anyway, he or the Pringles overpowered her —there are some bruises on her body to show that she put up a struggle—and then they probably tied a plastic bag over her head and waited for her to suffocate. Then they carried her down to the boat and left her there. They probably hoped it would be thought she'd committed suicide, without knowing, of course, that a letter saying that was just what she was going to do, and an empty bottle of Somnolin would be waiting in her bedroom."

"But when did that letter get written?" David asked. "How could Wellman do it, if he was asleep?"

"I think he woke up a few hours later and remembered what he'd planned to do," Ross said. "But the room was dark, so he didn't see his wife wasn't in her bed, and he slipped into the lounge and scribbled the few lines that were found next day and left the note on the dressing-table."

"You know, I heard what sounded like a struggle in the Pringles' house," Ian said, "and I thought I heard a woman scream, but with my hands tied I couldn't do anything but yell, which I did, but nobody took any notice of it. But I'll tell you one thing I'm sure of, Pete wasn't there. He came to the house soon after I got there and I recognized his voice, and they seemed to be talking about dumping me in the river, but Pete said if they did he'd give the whole show away. He said as long as I didn't know where I'd been they'd be safe, and that they should dope me and drive me back into town and dump me somewhere in the Australia Day crowds where there'd be too many people around for anyone to be sure of just what had happened. And that's what they did this morning. They didn't know, of course, that I'd recognized the clanking of the ferry. I wasn't dead certain that I was on Hindmarsh Island, but I was fairly sure."

"And have you got Slattery?" David asked.

"Not yet. He's got away. But we'll get him sooner or later, that's for sure. Meantime it happens we're in need of evidence against him. Mr. Gairdner's statement may be useful, but I gather he didn't actually see the man. The person who I think will break down and tell us all we need is Pete Wellman. Once we can convince him that his father really didn't murder his mother and that these friends of his did, I think he'll tell us everything he knows."

"But why did Andrew Wellman confess to killing his wife?" David asked.

"Because he thinks he did it. As I told you, he'd planned to do it, he doped the drink, he wrote the letter. But when he woke up in the morning he couldn't understand why his wife wasn't in her bed. He remembered what he'd done and he was sure she'd be there in the room with him, but she was missing. Then when she was found in the boat, he thought she must have managed to stagger out there, for some mysterious reason, before the drug knocked her out. Then he couldn't face what he'd done and told us the whole story. Only it just happens, through no fault of his own, not to be true."

"But can't you arrest him for anything?" Mrs. Rayne inquired. "After all, he *meant* to kill her."

Ross shook his head. "I doubt if you can arrest a man for having delusions about having committed a murder. And he can easily change his story at any time. No, I fancy he'll go free."

"And marry Eudora?" Rachel asked.

"Now there I'm afraid I can't help you, as I don't know the lady," Ross said. "Did she know what he was going to do? Is that why she took such offence when young Wellman started accusing her of having tried to poison Miss Gairdner? After all, it gave her a good excuse to leave and be miles away when the murder happened. Or was she perfectly innocent? Perhaps Mr. Gairdner can tell us what he thinks."

"What I *think!*" Ian clutched his head in both hands. "I'm not in much of a state for thinking at the moment. After what I've been through and after all you've been telling us—well, I'm not very clear about anything. Come and ask me that question in two or three days' time and perhaps I'll have some sort of answer for you. But it'll only be what I *think*, you understand, and that won't be much use to you, will it? I mean, I've no sort of evidence, one way or the other. But I'll tell you one thing, I've got a hell of a headache and what I'd like to do is to get back to my room and sleep off the remains of this drug, whatever it is they gave me. I don't mean, of course, that I don't want to be helpful, but if there's nothing much more I can do for you now, I really would like to go home. And I'd like to get out of these clothes I've been in since Friday and have a shower and some peace and quiet with Rachel. We've a lot to tell each other about things that haven't anything to do with murder."

Ross nodded with some appearance of sympathy. "Yes, of course. I'm sure the best thing for you to do is to take it easy. I'll be along to see you again tomorrow or the day after. Perhaps my own mind may be a bit clearer by then. You'll be needed at the inquest, of course, but you needn't worry about that for the moment. Now I'll be off myself. I'm glad, for Miss Gairdner's sake as well as yours, you've turned up safe and sound."

He stood up and went to the door. David let him out.

Coming back, he said, "I'll drive you and Rachel home, Ian. It's only round the corner, but you may find, when you try to walk, that it feels further than it is. Come along."

"And remember," Mrs. Rayne said, "if there's any way we can help, you've only to call us."

Ian thanked her, still with the slightly bewildered air of one who was not quite sure who she was or how she had come into his life, but Rachel thanked her, was kissed by her, then followed Ian and David to the door.

Ian walked fairly steadily but seemed glad to have David's arm to hold on to as they made for the lift, and after they had emerged from it, for his help to where his car was parked. He drove them the short distance to Bessborough Street and got out of the car with them, but Ian by now seemed to want to walk by himself through the barren little garden to the house. Excited barking from the other side of the front door greeted them.

Ian naturally had no key in his pockets, but Rachel found hers in her handbag. Turning to David, who was standing just behind her, she said, "What are we going to do about the dogs? Ian and I can look after them for the present, but I've no idea what we'll be going to do, I mean, whether we'll be staying in this house or what, so I can't say for sure what we can do about them."

"If I were you, I'd ask my mother about that," David

said. "She's involved with nearly all the good works in Adelaide and there's almost sure to be a group she knows about who look after unwanted pets."

"Poor things," Rachel said, "it somehow sounds so sad, just being unwanted. Actually I'm rather fond of Bungo and I think he likes me, but if I took him home with me it would mean leaving him for months in quarantine."

"But you aren't thinking of going home yet, are you?" David said quickly.

"No, but I suppose it's what I'll do sooner or later," she replied.

"Then wait a bit before you decide his fate," he said. "After all, when all this trouble's been cleared up, you might decide you'd like to see a bit of Australia. You never know, you might stay on for quite a while."

She met his eyes gravely. "Perhaps I might." Fitting her key into the door, she went on, "About your mother's invitation—"

"Oh, forget that," he interrupted. "That was only because we didn't like the idea of you staying in this house alone, but now Ian's here, of course it's different. You'll want to stay with him."

"And you'll go to Tasmania for your trout-fishing."

"I suppose I shall, unless the police want me to stay. I'll only be gone for two weeks, however, and I don't see why they should need me. But if Ian requires a chance to recuperate after what he's been through, Tasmania might be a very good place for him to go. Think about it."

"It's an idea. I'll talk to him about it."

"In any case, beginning now, I hope you have a happy visit in Australia."

That made her laugh, though she was not sure that it should.

"Thank you," she said.

"Goodbye."

"Goodbye."

He turned and walked back to his car.

As he drove away Rachel turned the key in the door and pushed it open. Bungo and Charlie came bounding out to greet her and Ian. Then Ian put an arm round her and kissed her warmly.

Smiling, he observed, "The man's in love with you."

She was about to state that having met the man for the first time only at four o'clock on Sunday morning, and in remarkably peculiar circumstances, this seemed unlikely, when it struck her that there was really no need for such pretences between her and Ian.

"I rather hope so," she said. "But now tell me, what's the truth about you and Eudora?"

"There's nothing much to tell," he said.

"You aren't engaged to be married?"

"We did talk about it once, but never settled anything."

"Then perhaps you were just part of a cover-up of her relationship with Andrew Wellman, because she knew there was murder in the offing. I wonder what the penalty is for planning to commit a murder which someone else carries out for you. The sergeant seemed to think you'd get off scot-free. What do you think Andrew Wellman will do now about his job?"

They had gone into the sitting-room and Rachel had dropped into a chair. Bungo, as his habit was, was doing his best to climb onto her lap.

"I imagine he'll have to resign from Ledyard Groome," Ian said. "Even if there's no penalty for what he's done, the story's sure to get around."

"And what will you do?"

"Stay on, I suppose, if they want me. If by any chance they decide to close down the branch here, I'll look for something else, if possible in Adelaide."

"You aren't thinking of going home?"

"Not for the present. And if by any chance you're going to be staying on—"

"Who said I was?"

He laughed and bent and stroked the boxer.

"Bungo, I believe, would welcome the idea. You and he could obviously become close friends. Now I'm going to get out of these clothes and have a shower and then we'll have a drink and talk about Aunt Christina and Edinburgh and perhaps even Tasmania."

About the author

E. X. Ferrars, who lives in England, is the author of more than forty works of mystery and suspense, including *The Crime and the Crystal, Root of All Evil, Something Wicked* and *Death of a Minor Character*. She was recently given a special award by the British Crime Writers Association for continuing excellence in the field of mystery writing.